THE CHAIN

JOY RICHARDS

BLOODHOUND
— BOOKS —

Print ISBN 978-1-913942-26-7

To Richard, Lily and Jack.

1

PAUL

Alice had wanted the wedding to be in Saint Lucia. There is a luxury resort on the west side of the island where you can walk down stone steps to two sandy beaches, connected by a narrow path through the jungle. She wanted to get married with her toes in the crystal-clear water, her hair and loose-fitting white linen dress blowing in the sweet breeze. Paul had wanted the reception in a marquee, in his parents' back garden in Kent. They could get married in the Saxon village church, then walk through the cobbled streets to his mum and dad's Arts-and-Crafts grade II-listed house and dance the night away in the garden. The second option being tens of thousands of pounds cheaper, and Paul being very emotionally attached to the idea, they ended up choosing Kent. They could always go to Saint Lucia for the honeymoon, she said back when they made their final decision. Except, of course, they ended up choosing Italy instead: in the summer, the only season for a proper English garden wedding, Saint Lucia on high alert for hurricanes.

That, in a nutshell, was the problem, Paul thought as he went through his weekly clean-up of the apartment. She wanted adventure, he wanted stability. At night, before going to bed, he would browse house prices on his phone while she looked at last-minute flight deals for Indonesia she never ended up booking. Of course it was obvious now, with the advantage of hindsight, that the relationship was never going to work. Irreconcilable differences, as he'd written in the wedding insurance form. Code for, she's packed up her things overnight and has dumped me by Facebook message on her way to the airport. On the way to Australia. Facebook message, not even a proper WhatsApp. She'd terminated her phone contract before leaving, so her only way of communicating with him was through Facebook on her laptop. For some reason, that was what had made him most angry. Not the fact she'd left him two months before their wedding, or the fact that this had been premeditated enough for her to look for a job in Melbourne, get hired and sort out all of her visa paperwork before she'd even started packing. It was the Facebook message.

Paul forced himself to take a deep breath. He was scrubbing his toilet, kneeling down in the small wedge of space between the shower cubicle and the door. He pushed his round glasses up the bridge of his nose, swiping his curly hair away from his damp forehead. Even now, two years later, he could start shaking when he thought of his anger. Hours of therapy later, he knew how to identify a wave of rage and stop it before it took his breath away. He still didn't like it, but he was becoming more and more able to think of other things and disrupt his destructive train of thought. This bathroom, for example. A joke, barely more than a closet, with cheap, pinkish lino covering the floor and mouldy paint on the ceiling. It had to be said, the bathroom went with the rest of his unbelievably shit apartment. A one-bedroom coffin, over a chicken shop that filled it with the overwhelming stench of grease during the day and an alien, deeply disturbing neon light. A nightmare flat, the first one he looked at, something he got in a hurry, never planning to spend more than a few nights there. He would spend most of his time at Alice's nice flat in Angel, but needed somewhere to go back to after nights out with his friends, and when Alice was on a night shift. He had not envisaged that he would spend two years living here full-time, going through a breakdown and spending more time "at home" than he ever had in his life. Ironic, considering how much he disliked his "home".

Why not move, was the first question anyone who stepped in asked. His parents, driving him back to London after a particularly bad couple of weeks when he'd retreated to the safety of his childhood bedroom. His remaining friends, who'd stuck by him through a rough couple of years and kept calling, inviting themselves over for a twenty-minute tea break to check on him. The handful of women he'd found on Bumble, all of whom seemed so nice, he felt genuinely awful using them to mop up his own pain. They did not seem to mind that he was using them, they probably also had their own thing going on. Before letting anyone into his meticulously clean but otherwise truly horrible and very soulless space, he prefaced it with a series of jokes, making sure his guests knew the flat was no reflection of him as a person. No art on the wall, stained furniture, something growing on the ceiling. Not what he thought his home would look like the year he turned thirty.

As one of the few heterosexual men truly interested in interior design, the mere sight of the place was punishment. Was he punishing himself? That was a question often explored by his various counsellors, his female friends, his mother and, most importantly, himself. Probably. But what for? He'd been a good boyfriend to Alice, and a good fiancé. He'd supported her through some tough times at work, brought her home-made brownies in the middle of long shifts in the hospital. He'd invested in her friends, at the expense of his own (which made it all the more impressive that so many of them had stood by him). His only fault, he realised, was that he had not been a good listener. He'd talked about children, how soon they could have them, how excited he was about the Shared Parental Leave scheme. Alice could go back to work whenever she felt ready, and he would take the rest of the year off. He might even go part-time after they'd had a couple. Alice's job as a doctor was likely to always pay more than his own in publishing – and he would relish the opportunity to look after the kids while they were small.

Alice, on the other hand, always seemed to talk about other things; friends who had taken a few years off their training to go work in Australia and New Zealand – amazing pay, away from the overstretched and underfunded NHS hospitals, and the possibility of travel after a few months of work. You can get to Bali in a few hours, she would say, her eyes glimmering with excitement. More and more, she dreamed about taking a year out, making some money with locum shifts at the local hospital and then taking off to go travelling for a few months. South-east Asia was her latest obsession: hopping a train through Vietnam, north to south, and then hiking her way through Cambodia before recuperating on a white sandy beach in Thailand. In her defence, her daydreams always included Paul, tagging along for the ride. But more and more, he would sound like a backpack she would take along more than a travel companion. If he'd listened better, he would have been able to see it coming.

Paul stood up, neatly storing his bathroom cleaning spray and sponge on top of the cabinet. As he turned towards the door, he hit his shin against the basin.

"Fuck!" He stretched his arm out for balance and leaned onto the sink, getting the sleeve of his shapeless grey jumper sodden with grimy soap water. "Fuck," he said again. *This flat is killing me*, he thought. *I need to move.*

For some reason, he had always envisaged the next step in his life consisting of moving in with someone. He and Alice were going to buy a place together after the wedding. She did not want to add to the wedding stress by looking for houses, but he couldn't wait. He'd spent hours on his phone, connected on all the house-search apps, scouring listings for their First Home Together. Their friends thought it was a bit weird they hadn't moved in together already, but Alice worked odd hours and they had wanted to preserve their own independent circle of friends. He had quite liked the idea of getting married and of their whole lives changing, transforming from one day to the next. While in practice they spent the majority of their evenings, nights and weekends together, moving in was going to be different. Their things would be kept in the same place. They would share things like the microwave and the vacuum, they would pool their kitchen implements and allocate closet space. And if they bought the place, they could decorate it how they pleased. At night, his face lit by the ethereal glow of his phone, he would pick out houses he liked, and imagine their shared life living there. Each house came with its own set of imaginary circumstances. He even had two he had saved on his phone, and was toying with the idea of showing Alice.

One was a semi-detached in Forest Hill, slightly falling apart but with a garden filled with apple trees that just so happened to be in bloom when the photographs were taken. It had four bedrooms, and peeling green shutters. Room for a growing family. There was a space out front to park a car: he could see a second-hand sensible vehicle propped there, waiting to take them camping or to the beach. The second option was a flat in Dulwich with a tiny roof terrace. A starter home, a cool hangout for their child-free years. They would host long boozy candlelit dinners for their (her?) friends, and get a cat. Both properties had been sold for well over a year. Paul would sometimes think of them, of the people who had ended up putting in an offer and what their lives looked like, on the set of his imaginary lives. Was there a young couple in the tiny flat? It could have just as easily been sold to a bachelor, unaware he was trampling over someone else's dreams of marital bliss.

He did know who was in the Forest Hill house, because he had stalked it. About a year after the break-up, at the height of his struggle, Paul had taken the overground from West Croydon on a wet afternoon. He didn't get off at Forest Hill, for some reason that seemed creepy and stalkerish. Instead, he waited for the next stop, Honor Oak Park. He then walked back along the leafy streets that were presumably once a forest until he found it. He did not have to use his deductive powers to ascertain who lived there, because they were all outside carrying in what looked like rugby kit from the car. Two parents, black, in their early forties. Two teenage boys, tall and muscular, wearing mud-soaked red shorts and jerseys, carrying their boots carefully in their hand as they crossed the threshold. The shutters had been repainted white, which looked better than the original green, and the grass in the front had been mowed, which made the house look rather smart.

His therapist had not been impressed with that story. That was not the behaviour of someone looking to move on, staring at strangers peacefully living in a house where you never even went for a viewing. Pretending to be looking for an address on the other side of the street, so you could walk past a few times and catch more details of their ordinary, happy life. Which rooms had been claimed by the boys, blue Chelsea trinkets peering from the windows. Whether or not they had knocked through the front room to make the kitchen open space.

After that, Paul got the message. He uninstalled the house-search apps from his phone. He worked hard to stop thinking about other people's lives, and start thinking about his. A few months later, he took a whole five weeks off work and went on a lone-wolf trip to Croatia, Montenegro, Macedonia and, ultimately, Greece. Various friends came to join him, one for a whole week of hiking, a couple for a long weekend at the beach. He went parasailing, rented a scooter to drive through the dusty country lanes of Crete, and took a five-day intensive diving course in a tiny Croatian village. His parents caught up with him on the last leg of his trip, and they all stayed in a posh resort on a tiny island. Lying by the pool sipping a cold beer with his dad, Paul realised he hadn't thought about Alice for a couple of days.

On his return to London, Paul started looking for a new job. He was due a promotion, but at his tiny company, opportunities were few and far between. His boss had been supportive during the whole ordeal, but his breakdown certainly hadn't put him on the radar as a reliable prospect for more senior roles. It was time to move on. With far more ease than anticipated, he found himself at a much larger, scarier, publishing company. There were more people in his department than at the whole of his old company. His work was harder, but he enjoyed it more. There were also more people his age, and he made a few work friends. At his old company, he had been limited to friendly acquaintances, people to have lunch with but who he would never choose to spend time with outside of work. Here, he found his little tribe of like-minded people.

His university friends were close, but lived very different lives. They were getting married, settling down, one or two were even having babies. Some were talking about leaving the city for a more relaxed pace of life. With his new friends, they went to pretentious hipster wine tastings and plagued every midweek comedy open mic night in south-east London. They sat outside fancy cafes at the weekend sipping flat whites and talking about books. One of them, a tall, skinny girl with dyed red hair the colour of blood oranges, kissed him while waiting for the night bus after a late pub night. Her bus came and she ran off and, at least seemingly, she was so drunk she completely forgot all about it by the morning.

That was convenient, as Paul was not ready to date. The Bumble girls made him feel more sad than anything else, and he seemed to have become impotent in the feelings department. While physically he was still very much able, he seemed to have lost the ability to fancy women. That was not uncommon, his counsellor had said, and it would go away by itself with time and hard work. He diverted his energy towards trying to improve himself. He signed up to a gym, something he had never dreamt of doing, and within a few months had developed new and unexpected muscles. He signed himself up to various free classes, from oil painting (a disaster), to Greek for beginners (frustrating), to Thai cookery (outstanding).

In all this, his old flat seemed to be more and more inadequate for his life. It was too small to have friends over: there was only really space for two (skinny) people at the small table in the kitchen area and the bed was visible from every corner of the apartment. It was embarrassing, especially now more of his friends cared about such things as decor, either because they were artistic or just older and more able to better provide for themselves. It was very cheap, which was good, but with his new job Paul could easily afford to pay a bit more. Plus, he still had his share of the deposit for the home he was going to buy with Alice, and the insurance reimbursement for the wedding that never happened. Really, he had no excuse not to buy.

That's where the issues started. Moving, buying, in a way acknowledged the finality of it all. Alice was not coming back. His first proper home was not to be one he shared with her.

Furthermore, and perhaps worse, there was no girlfriend to replace her. He was not going to move out of his crappy apartment to move in with a new woman, adventure beckoning. He was going to need to move out just to move back in with himself. Not a new life, but a continuation of this one. On the other hand, what other choice did he have?

2

FLORENCE

"F uck," Florence said as she walked into the kitchen. "I hate this house." Tim, age two, was oblivious to his mother's swearing, curled up on the nursing chair in the corner glued to a tablet blasting an episode of *Paw Patrol*. The dog, upstairs, mercifully stopped his insistent barking. The rest of the scene looked like a "before" picture of a house transformation show. Brightly coloured plastic toys were strewn across the floor of the kitchen-diner, and two towering stacks of mail and miscellaneous papers covered the surface of the dining table. On top of the papers, the remainders of lunch: a big plate for Mummy, a small bowl for Tim, with the gnawed carcasses of three broccoli florets browning in the afternoon air. The kitchen counters were covered in various kitchen equipment that could not find room in the already overstuffed cupboards: a steamer, a blender, a bag of sandwich bread, a massive spice rack, a tower of baby bottles and plastic cups. The counters were also dirty with the splattered remains of dinner, pasta sauce congealed on the wooden countertops and little crumbs of a salad wilting in the crevices near the stove. A mess. Like the rest of the house.

She hated that house. Florence's heart sank as she heard

herself say it, but it was true. She was spending more and more time outside, allegedly "for Tim" but really so she wouldn't have to look at it. What was so heartbreaking was that until very recently she had loved her house. It had been her source of pride and joy, her secret obsession. The day she'd found it, she knew that was "it". She and John had been recently engaged and looking for a place to buy together after sharing a flat for a little over a year. She would go on exploratory viewings and weed out weak candidates, reserving only the really promising properties for a second viewing with John, who was putting in long hours at the firm.

She had loved the look of the house online, and she'd come early to scope it out. In the middle of a long row of Victorian terraces it stood, a baby-pink house with the bright white door, clad in wisteria with a front garden full of pebbles. The wisteria had not actually been in bloom when she first came, but the lime-green leaves surrounded the front door like a magical passageway to Narnia. Over the door, a panel of what she was pretty sure was an authentic, 1920s stained-glass panel: an intricate pattern of purple iris flowers and leaves, glistening in the sun. She didn't even wait for the estate agent to come and show her the inside: she got out her phone and texted John straight away. "This is it," she said, in the dramatic tone he used to find so funny. "I've found it."

After they moved, Florence took a whole month of unpaid leave (does it still count as unpaid leave if the art gallery where you work barely pays you?) to sort out the house. It was, in many ways, the best month of her life. She would wake up at six and slowly drink her coffee while wandering the rooms, her eyes and mind filled with projects for the new day. She resisted the temptation to knock down the wall between the front room and the kitchen-diner and, instead, turned it into a cosy snug for two. She scoured the flea markets for vintage tiles and for period furniture: a crushed velvet love seat, a Victorian dining table with Eau-de-Nil legs, a claw-foot white bathtub that barely fitted in the only bathroom. The tiny garden, miraculously, had needed no work. It was pure perfection. Entirely paved in natural stone, with a thick border of overgrown lush roses that filled it with a heady scent July through October. She found a small wrought-iron garden table and matching chairs for it, and her work was done.

For their first three summers in the house, Florence and John spent every evening sat on the impractical garden chairs, drinking very cold white wine and savouring the scent of the roses. They had friends over for huge meals of succulent lamb tagine or just delivery pizzas, everyone piling around the dining room table and laughing at stories from mishap holidays and grotesque bosses. It was their love nest, where they came to find each other in their crazy London lives. When they came back from their many honeymoons (only one was actually called a honeymoon, but they all felt like it), they would shake the sweat and tiredness at the door and sigh, glad to be home. Fresh off the plane from Morocco, Colombia, Nepal or "just" Berlin, they would giggle like teenagers as they took all their clothes off and recuperated in bed, often for a whole afternoon that slowly turned into a late late night.

An insistent whining brought Florence back to reality. Tim had finished his juice and wanted some more. The large expanding stain on the nursing chair seemed to suggest a spillage, but she chose to ignore it. She filled up his plastic sippy cup with sugary orange liquid and returned him to the kaleidoscopic world of his tablet. Not how she thought she'd parent her two-year-old, but she did not have the energy to do anything else. She had to get the house at least a little under control, and she could feel her swollen feet throbbing underneath her large belly.

"Leave the housework," said the mummy blogs. "Sleep when the baby sleeps. Let others help you". This advice seemed to conjure the image of a whole village of long-haired, soft-spoken women coming over with pots of steaming stew and staying for an hour or so to clean your house, while you napped upstairs with your tender child. Of course, that was all bullshit. People may bring over some brownies and offer to run the hoover around for you the week your baby is actually born, but nobody will offer to tidy your disgusting house on a boiling Wednesday afternoon twenty-four months down the line. And living in a disaster zone is not as restful as the mummy bloggers seemed to suggest. In fact, it sucks. I need to snap out of it, Florence told herself.

She cleared a spot from a cluster of Duplo blocks and lay down on the floor, the wooden floorboards cool under her skin. There were piles of clean laundry on the dining table chairs, spluttered with sauce from the previous night's dinner. Just behind that was an even more depressing sight, the conservatory. They used to refer to it as the "conservatory" in quotation marks, with an amused chuckle, because it was so small it was unclear why it had ever been built. Maybe it was vanity on behalf of the owners – who thought it would sound grand to have a conservatory, no matter how small. Who knows. They had thought it charming when they'd first moved in, yet another little quirky mark of their little quirky house.

For a while, John thought it could be his "home office". He soon discovered it was freezing in the winter and horrifyingly hot in the summer. To make matters worse, the only table they could fit in there was too small for John to sit comfortably. The idea of the home office was abandoned, and it soon turned into a receptacle of various rubbish they were too busy to bring to the charity shop. It was overcome with baby clothes that were too small, adult clothes Florence was too pregnant for, a spare kitchen mixer, a broken tricycle, and the hoover.

Past the conservatory was the garden. Once an oasis, it was now marred by a bright yellow mud kitchen Tim hated to play with (no mummy bloggers mentioned what to do if your toddler has a veritable horror of getting dirty) and a very expensive paddling pool, complete with inflatable flamingo and palm tree, which stood flaccid, chewed on by the dog.

Of course, the dog. The dog was John's idea after three years of marriage. They had talked about having babies, and he wanted to "test it out" with a dog first. Plus, wouldn't it be great for the kids to grow up with a pet? Florence was so giddy at the idea of having a baby, so broody and so desperate for John to be broody too (you're not allowed to be desperate when you are twenty-seven, so she had no leverage) she would have agreed to a pet tarantula. She was more of a cat person herself, but she liked dogs well enough. However, there was one thing she would not compromise on: it had to be a rescue dog, from the shelter. John's heart was set on a chocolate Labrador from a breeder. Uncharacteristically, she would not budge. In the end he caved, and they spent an amazing afternoon at the Battersea Puppy Home, playing with puppies until they found their guy. He looked just like a chocolate Labrador, but with a shorter stoutier snout. They fell in love instantly, or rather, Florence fell in love and John agreed to give the dog a chance. "You can always come back if the adoption doesn't work out," said the friendly volunteer at the shelter who sensed a difference in opinion. So they stocked up on leashes and bowls at the shelter shop and brought the dog home.

They named him Spencer, and he took up residence under the kitchen table. John started taking him on long runs in the morning before work and no mention was ever made again of purebred Labradors. Curiously, the more Spencer stayed, the more John grew to love him and the less Florence liked him. He was a good dog, friendly and well trained, but he was nothing like a baby and that's what Florence was aching for. John seemed so content with the dog, he stopped talking about children and she could not help but wonder, as she watched her husband wrestle Spencer on the floor, whether the dog had filled a child-sized hole in his heart.

Spencer came in from upstairs and loudly lapped up some water from his bowl. Tim let out a shriek of delight at the sight of his shaggy friend. In spite of her general sense of feeling overwhelmed, Florence couldn't help but smile. They were so sweet: the patchy shaggy dog and the yellow-haired angelic child, looking at each other with untold fondness. Neither of them could speak properly, but they both knew they were best friends already. Untold adventures awaited. Between the two of them, they had already destroyed her Moroccan rug, which had been replaced by a soulless IKEA number with yellow squiggles on it. What a team. She slowly got up, wary of her second-trimester heftiness, and made her way over to Tim. She stroked his hair as he returned to watching his show.

"Will the baby like my shows?" Tim asked without looking away from the screen. He had immediately internalised the idea of a baby growing in Mummy's tummy, and talked about it as though it was already an established fact of life. He'd studied the book they'd got him. "I'm going to be a big brother!" and decided the whole thing was going to be fun. He had no interest in how the baby was going to get out of Mummy's tummy, and frankly it was just as well. After labouring in that very kitchen and needing a last-minute hospital transfer when the home-birth plan did not pan out as well as she had hoped, Florence was going to cool it slightly with the hippie-dippie stuff. She had rehired the same doula out of politeness and a fear of awkwardness: she ran her mummy-and-me group and would definitely notice as Florence started turning up more and more pregnant.

"Of course she will, my love," Florence replied, feeling dizzy at the thought of another baby, an actual baby girl strapped to her chest, coming along on their daytime adventures. Unlike her son, Florence still struggled to comprehend she was going to have another baby. The first time round, she got pregnant after months of trying, hoping, inspecting endless pregnancy tests and analysing every little twinge in her stomach. The thought of being pregnant had been on her mind for so long, the feeling of the baby growing inside her was but a mere extension of that. She felt as though she had willed him into existence from thin air, a miracle effort of love and determination. This baby was different. This baby was a mistake.

What woman gets pregnant the same week she is going to leave her husband? She had a whole list of excuses in her head, but she never felt any of them were good enough. Sex had been so infrequent after Tim was born. It had not been easy, through the long nights of co-sleeping, the fifteen months of breastfeeding, and her deep embarrassment at her once very slender frame now clouded in odd lumps of fat. The idea of getting pregnant by accident had seemed ridiculous: it had taken them seven months to get pregnant the first time, in spite of Florence scientifically tracking her cycles and them having sex every other day, religiously, like an act of faith. John thought of it as a matter of certainty, like finishing a puzzle, completing their incomplete perfect family with another child or two. It wasn't that she didn't want to, but she simply couldn't imagine it. Contraception had seemed like a problem for someone else, women with healthier marriages, smaller tummies and generally a more buxom disposition. And yet, there it had been, in the bathroom of a Starbucks with no toilet paper, her baby girl waving at her through two thin pink lines.

Florence had been at one of her many mummy-and-me groups. This one was informal, five mums who had met at antenatal class still bonded by their shared experiences of motherhood and love for the NCT. Hilariously, they now mostly discussed husbands. Their petty squabbles, how they forgot instructions, or didn't listen, or spent too much time on their phone. Today, in Starbucks, it'd been the turn of Olivia, a fat cheerful woman with two-under-two whose husband had, bewilderingly, bought a PlayStation. While the other women sipped their drinks and ate their cookies and reacted with the expected coos of disbelief and righteous rage ("what IS wrong with him?"), Florence had sat back and resisted the urge to scream. That's annoying for you, Olivia, she'd thought. My husband fucks his receptionist and doesn't even respect me enough to text her on a secret phone. It's all there, for anyone to see. All I had to do was pick up his phone to google how long chicken should be in the oven.

I thought we were going through a scheduled tough time, me absorbed in motherhood, him in his career. Everyone told me this was to be expected, that he may sleep on the sofa for a few months to get some rest while I stayed up with our baby. That he may feel a little left out, but that deep down he understood and loved me. That I may not feel close to him now, but that I would again as soon as the baby would start sleeping through the night. But he wasn't "getting rest". He was up all night texting her, and not just about where to meet and how horny he was, but about his hopes and dreams. His little triumphs and bad days, his worries about his dad's diabetes and John's funny stories about his weekend away with his brother. His whole inner life, of which I knew nothing, like a stranger. And now I'm pregnant. So sorry, Olivia, but I win. Go me.

Florence had never much cared for a career. She'd had jobs, obviously, and a degree. But that was not the long-game. She had always seen herself as a mum, her employment a short footnote in the "before" section of her life, and perhaps in the "after", when she may pick up a couple of days working in a lovely shop. Like her own mother before her, she was furiously cultured, a declared feminist and very much of a housewife at heart. A homemaker, as she liked to think about it. A maker of home, of happiness, of calm. Of cakes, even. The idea of getting divorced wasn't just unappealing, it threatened the existence of her very identity.

A housewife implies a husband. She might have hesitated to leave him if it had just been the sex. After all, the sex in their marriage was now bad and rare. More often than not, they both kept their T-shirts on and the light off. But in those texts was a whole life, a whole person she did not know anymore. The thought of his emotional infidelity made her feel repulsed by her own sad existence, her ships-in-the-night marriage.

She had to leave. She made plans: where to go, what to do. She could stay with her parents for a few months. There was a great local childminder some of her friends had used; that could free her up to look for part-time work. It was a comforting plan, one that gave her strength. And then she got pregnant again, and felt all the choices being taken away from her.

She'd thrown the pregnancy test in the bin. After the mummy group had ended she'd gone home and cooked chicken piccata for dinner from one of her collection of beautiful recipe books. When John had made it home, they'd exchanged a pleasant few words and then had eaten quietly while watching TV. They were binge-watching famous shows they'd missed, and had only just tackled the second season of *The Wire*. After dinner he'd watched some rugby highlight videos on his phone, while she'd tidied. They'd watched another two episodes of *The Wire* and she'd gone to sleep, with Tim. "I'll do some work and catch up with you," he'd said, and she'd marvelled at herself for ever believing him. He didn't even have his laptop. Like a magic trick, once you know where the cheese wire is, you can no longer believe in the floating top hat.

And there she was, four months later, clearing up her downstairs and feeling the numbness rush through her toes. John had been, she had to make herself believe that, genuinely thrilled about the pregnancy. What was upsetting was that he was not surprised. He had always taken the next baby, like the rest of his scripted life, as a matter of course. That's just what happens next. You date a girl for a few years in your twenties, so you propose. You propose, so you get married. You get married, wait a few years, go on trips, maybe get a pet. Then you have a baby, no sooner than twenty-eight and no later than thirty-four. Then you have one more, possibly of the opposite gender. If you cannot manage the right gender, you may have one more. You move to the countryside and commute in, so there is enough room for everyone. Trade the cramped dwellings designed for pint-sized Victorians for a "forever home".

Florence thought about their neat life, correctly. Life is easy, you just need to do what's next.

3

CLAIRE

"Oh dear," Claire said out loud to no one in particular, a note of melancholy in her voice. "I love this house." Marmalade the cat jumped down from the kitchen counter and scurried off in a hurry, the long hair on his erect tail swishing around like a flag in the wind. Claire dunked her empty mug in the soapy water while looking outside. The garden glistened with the morning dew. Beyond it, the fields of Surrey, arranged like in a Turner painting, blushing in the mist of the early morning.

"What did you say?" her husband, Michael, asked as he limped into the kitchen.

"Oh, nothing," she said, startled. She hadn't heard him come down the stairs. While in generally great shape for seventy-one, her hearing on the left side was not good. "Just that I love this house."

He reached over and put his arms over her shoulders, dressing gown against dressing gown. "I know," he said, "I love it too." His speech impediment had got worse over the years and made it hard for some people to understand him, but she could barely notice it.

"Do you remember when we moved in here?" he asked, although that was rhetorical. They had a framed and rather faded photo of that day in the hallway, he with a dark bushy beard, she with long straight unruly hair bleached by the sun. A tiny baby in a white romper in her lap.

"We were so young," she replied, turning round and nestling in his hug. "I was probably pregnant with Aaron and didn't even know it."

"Were you?" he leaned slightly back to look her in the eyes. After forty-some years together, he still couldn't get enough of her symmetrical, perfectly oval face.

"I must have been! We moved in July, Jacob had just turned one. Aaron was born in March, so I must have been pregnant and not known it." How had Michael not figured this out by now?

"Was he? Wait, how old was he when we left for Kenya?"

She giggled. Her absent-minded man, one of the sharpest minds she'd ever known, but unsure of his son's birthday. "He was six months old, dear."

"Blimey. We were slightly irresponsible, weren't we?"

She kissed him lightly. "It worked out for us, didn't it, love?"

He held her tightly, with a sudden squeeze. Thinking about the past made him feel vulnerable. "It most certainly did."

"Right," she continued, in a matter-of-fact voice, "go set the table and find the paper. I'll bring breakfast through in a minute."

"Aye aye, capitaine." He disappeared in the general direction of the dining room. A pot of oats, with berries and peach slices, bubbled away on the mint-green Aga. Coffee was brewing in the French press, the second of the day. There was fresh orange juice in the glass jug in the fridge. Everything was going to be all right. Yet Claire felt her eyes well up, thinking about her kitchen, and her home.

They had needed a haven so badly on that day when they'd moved in, a nest of safety in an unsafe world. They'd just come back from their first joint posting in the Foreign Office, in Jerusalem, which was no easy placement in the early eighties. They'd met in Beirut only four years earlier, on what had been the first ever post for both of them. They'd fallen in love immediately, urgently and rather spectacularly. She'd actually been on a first date with someone else when they met, a Navy liaison officer who was handsome and well spoken and just generally a good choice. She took one look at Michael, with his hippie looks and even hippier political opinions, and decided they should spend every single minute together for the rest of their lives. He very much agreed.

They married with five guests at the Lewisham Registry Office two days after they'd returned to England. After that, Jerusalem. A place she'd loathed for the first six months and was heartbroken to leave three years later. Their first home together, in a crumbling apartment in West Jerusalem with bars on the windows and red geraniums in terracotta pots on the tiled floor. It was where she'd fallen in love with cooking, thanks to a wonderful Orthodox housekeeper who would come in every morning with a new recipe for her, scribbled in pointy handwriting on a piece of second-hand baking parchment. It was where Jacob was born.

They'd returned home again feeling less at home than ever. Their possessions filled three suitcases and two cardboard boxes in Claire's mother's attic. They had a baby, a little bundle of giggles who would stare at them with his toothless wide smile in serene expectation. They felt out of place, like they were foreigners in their own land. London, her extended playground in her university years, felt more foreign than anything else. They needed a home to call home. Surrey seemed to beckon with its home-county appeal: they took the train down for a sunny weekend, staying in the rooms over a country pub and roamed the villages while eating ice creams. It took them several such weekends to find the house; once they'd found it, it was home.

Michael put down his newspaper as she came into the room, carrying the breakfast tray. He poured her a coffee, a tiny gesture to show her his immense affection. Her thoughts were all over her face.

"We just knew, didn't we?" he said, wiping a steel grey strand of hair from her tanned forehead and handing her the filled cup. "From the moment we pulled into the front drive."

"We were driving? I don't think we had a car back then."

"It was Dad's. Remember? Jacob had been teething and it was a nightmare to push him around in the stroller."

Ah yes. The faded station wagon. The baby crawling across the back seats. You probably went to prison for that now. Michael was right though, the moment they saw the house, they knew they were home. Two months later, they'd moved in. That was another funny day.

"We really didn't have that much stuff, did we?" She chuckled. "Remember? It was ridiculous. This great big Georgian house, huge yew trees out front and there we come in our T-shirts with holes and our tiny pile of possessions."

"You put a stop to that pretty quickly, didn't you, darling?" He helped himself to the porridge. The smell of freshly grated cinnamon and peach filled the dining room as he lifted the lid.

She smiled. This house had turned her into more of a materialist. There hadn't been a posting, a holiday or a weekend away that hadn't seen her return with some item of decor. "That wasn't until later though. The house was still pretty bare when we went to Kenya."

He shook his head and rolled his eyes with exaggerated discontent. "Bare? Bare? You're crazy, woman. I remember coming back from Kenya and the house feeling like Buckingham Palace."

He was right, it had. After a tough and absolutely wonderful four years in rural Kenya, coming home had felt like a thousand pounds of dead weight had been lifted off of their shoulders. They had three children by the time they stepped back in the black-and-white tiled hallway: Jacob was six, Aaron was four and Elijah was about to turn two. They'd had proper travel trunks this time. In one of them was the draft of Claire's first book, typed on a crumbling 1940s typewriter she had found in the closet of their old colonial home. Michael had carried Jacob on his shoulders, and delicately holding an asleep Aaron over his arm. He'd been a giant then, a benevolent Goliath. Endlessly strong. Before his strength was taken away.

He carried on, in his cracked voice that made it so hard for anyone other than his family to understand him. "And after that, you started with the animals. All of bloody Noah's Ark. The cats, the dogs, the hamsters, the lizards, the mice, the chickens, the goats." He sounded furious, but his eyes were glistening with laughter. Teasing Claire had always been his favourite pastime.

"You're being ridiculous," she quipped back, "we've never had goats."

"Are you serious? We did, too, have a goat in that very garden." He gestured with his long arm in the general direction of the outdoors.

"We fostered a sheep once if that's what you mean," she replied coolly, sipping her coffee to hide her infectious grin.

"I apologise. Sheep. Totally different."

"Well, the children loved it."

Michael could no longer mask his large smile "They did, my love, they certainly did."

"Wild as they were. Monstrous boys." Four boys, by the end of it, all two years apart and with bounds of energy. The animals had kept them busy during their scattered years in Surrey, when they had to contend with the monotony of English life. An abrupt change from their long stints in some of the most exotic corners of the world.

"I got a text from Jacob this morning," Michael said, tucking into his porridge. "They're thinking of coming down the weekend after next. And they can make the Skype Quiz."

"Oh, that's great. This has me thinking... I suppose if we do end up moving back to London we'll be able to have quiz night in person again!"

"Like the good old days!"

They both took a pause to drink coffee and think back at their weekly quiz nights as a young family. They had taken the children all over the world with them living in disparate accommodation: from lush villas to decrepit plantation houses, and even a dodgy penthouse apartment in Dar es Salaam. They'd spent years in Surrey and years in areas torn by conflict, famine or disease. But no matter what, Tuesday night was quiz night. The stack of questions continually replenished, by buying them when in England or by getting friends and strangers to write new questions on chocolate-stained index cards. In the late nineties, the big cardboard box with all the questions had been replaced by a computer programme on the clunky family laptop, and in recent years by a fancy app on their phones.

As the children left home for university, quiz night had started happening over Skype. Sometimes the team was not complete, as the kids found themselves new adventures. Sometimes it was just Claire and Michael. Sometimes they brought along friends. Significant others came and went from the screens, often first introduced to the family through the webcam. Eventually, spouses became a fixture on Tuesday night, three wonderful wives and one wonderful husband. The grandkids were too small to take part, as the oldest was six, but there would be a time soon when they may well start interjecting with the answers. Often hilariously wrong, sometimes strangely accurate. Kids learn about all sorts of things while adults are not paying attention. You can tell so much about how a child is learning if you play a quiz game with them.

As the accidental home-schooling mum of four, Claire knew that all too well. Most of their peers left their children back in England at boarding school while the parents were posted around the world. Claire and Michael couldn't even think of it. So, Claire co-opted a large surface wherever they went – a table, a countertop, a large rug on the floor, and taught them as best as she knew how. The local state school had been very understanding, letting the boys tap in and out as they came and went. Every year they came back, they sat a test to see if they were behind. Every single time, they tested at least one year ahead of where they should have been. The school let them all skip one year ahead, but no more. Claire understood. School was not just learning, it was socialisation. A brilliant eleven-year-old in a classroom of fifteen-year-olds would not learn anything about how to make friends.

Like many families that move around a lot, they were close. In fact, until they were all in middle school the children often spoke a sort of language they had made up: part English, part Swahili, part funny mouth sounds. The secret code of an unbreakable tribe of boys, a band of brothers who slept, breathed and ran in unison. Anywhere they went, they were with their best friends. They begged their parents to knock down the wall between two of the bedrooms in the house in Surrey and put bunk beds in, so they could all sleep together even though there was enough space for each of them to have their own room.

When Jacob went to university, the other boys looked lost,

traumatised, until he rang them in secret every night, telling them all about the beers and the girls. After Jacob left, Aaron, Elijah and Gideon all followed in his footsteps to study medicine. They schemed and plotted until they all found themselves together again, in Oxford, Jacob doing his first year of foundation training, Aaron and Elijah having joined the clinical school from intercalated degrees from Bristol and Manchester respectively and Gideon as an undergraduate. They all rented a big house together in a leafy part of town, and yet they would all up sticks and come down to Surrey for one weekend a month, come hell or high water.

"Do you remember when the boys all used to live in that weird house in Oxford?" Michael asked, and Claire marvelled once again at his ability to follow her convoluted train of thought.

"They loved that," she answered, remembering how slightly jealous she was of their new home away from home.

"I wonder if London may feel that way in a few years. If we move up there," he said, pausing for a sip of orange juice, "and if Aaron and Penelope settle there once they come back. We could be all together again."

"They probably will," she replied. "That's where all the jobs seem to be. And that's where Gideon, Jacob and Elijah are. You know you can't keep those boys apart."

Aaron and Penelope. Taking after their parents, Aaron and Gideon had both spent a significant portion of their time trying to save various God-forsaken corners of the world. Aaron as a doctor with MSF, Gideon as a journalist after he'd abandoned his medical studies in favour of a more creative career. Gideon had come home the day Melissa, his long-term girlfriend, texted him she was pregnant, interrupting an assignment reporting on electoral controversies in Uganda. There was a hint of criticism for his parents in his choices, an indication that his own ramshackle upbringing had not always been the thrilling adventure they had intended it to be.

Aaron, on the other hand, had seemed to want to replicate his own childhood. He married his fellow MSF physician, Penelope, and they seemed to relish their nomadic life across the continents. Then, suddenly, they declared they were tired, and ready for something else. They were landing back in Heathrow in two months, looking for jobs in England. London, probably. Perhaps this time Claire and Michael should be the ones who joined the boys. London was calling.

"Are you sad?" Michael asked, his eyes suddenly sharp over his coffee moustache.

"A little."

"Is it the house?"

"Oh, it's so stupid," she said, her voice cracking with sudden emotion. "It's only a big square pile of bricks after all. But it's meant so much to us for most of our lives."

He looked surprised. "I suppose that was most of our lives, you know. It's weird thinking I've now spent most of my life with you, kid."

She giggled. He knew how to cheer her up. "Do you know what I mean though? I feel so superficial for caring about a house like it's a person."

"Of course you do! And we don't have to go anywhere you don't want to." He had been gently coaxing her into thinking about moving for weeks. She knew it was the right thing to do.

"I know! But you're right, this is stupid. It's the two of us and poor little Marmalade in a five-bedroomed house hours away from all our family. It doesn't make sense!"

"And the kids can't keep on coming down like they did before," he said, repeating a long-laboured point. "They have families of their own, things to do. They can't keep coming down one weekend every four like they used to."

"Of course." She waved her hand around. The tears were mounting at the back of her throat, and that made her angry with herself. "I know. It's only right, time for us to go and be useful grandparents."

"There are other benefits too." Michael had started his sermon and was not to be derailed off it. "We'll be in town, with all our friends from the good old days. We can go eat in interesting places, as opposed to just the Bistro Night at the Horse and Groom. We can go to the theatre more. And it will be so much easier with my hospital appointments."

Every five weeks, like clockwork, Michael and Claire took the train into town for a morning appointment with the Neurology team at St Thomas's Hospital. They were repetitive and never found anything new, but they would never ease up. When you have had a bullet fished out of your brain, millimetres away from the really important grey stuff, you need to keep on top of it. After the appointment, they always walked on Southbank up to a little pizza restaurant done up to look like a pastel beach hut. They had lunch, and a glass of red wine. Then they kept walking towards London Bridge station, looking past the grey water at the city in front of them.

Sometimes they met up with friends for dinner, sometimes they took the train straight back. Sometimes Claire went shopping in Oxford Street and left Michael perusing the shelves at Foyle's. Throughout the day, they spoke very little. They both never thought they would get to have more days like these.

Michael was shot on 25 November 1992 in Rwanda. The circumstances of his involvement had never been declassified, which irritated Claire since it really wasn't that big of a deal. By that time, they were no longer civil servants. Michael worked for a humanitarian organisation, and Claire's books were already selling well enough to constitute a job. They had been living in Mwanza, on Lake Victoria, working with Rwandan refugees.

One evening, someone from their old lives, someone in military intelligence had knocked on the door. There were hostages. Someone had to negotiate, and the only person with the necessary credibility in both camps was Michael.

Claire was chopping up tomatoes for dinner, and listening to Elijah read his book report on Nathaniel Hawthorne's *The Scarlett Letter*. She didn't really have time to process what was going on, Michael rushing through the house to grab his camera, the other man waiting at the door while smoking a cigarette. Michael plonked a hurried kiss on the top of her forehead and in a heartbeat he was gone.

Claire blinked. It still felt raw, after all these years.

"I know, my love," she said, the tears dry. "I know. It's time to move on."

4

ALEX

Alex looked over the small squalid airport hotel room and drew in a deep breath. Man, he wanted to go home. He'd missed his connecting flight from Singapore and was stuck in Frankfurt until the next day. He threw his suitcase on the double bed in frustration. It bounced off, crashing on the thin dirty carpet. *Fuck.*

Thankfully the laptop hadn't broken. He opened FaceTime on his phone and pressed the little picture of Sarah's. After a couple of seconds, she picked up on the other end.

"Hello!" she said from their flat in London. "Have you landed yet?"

"I'm stuck in Frankfurt," he said, plainly, trying to contain the disappointment on his face. He'd not seen her in over a week, and he ached to hold her. It sounded dramatic and rather stupid, but it was the truth.

She frowned. "Really? That is so annoying!" she said, while looking at an indeterminate point over the phone.

"Right," he said, underwhelmed and slightly hurt by her reaction. "I should get home tomorrow around ten. I'll work from home the rest of the day, I'm shattered."

"I'm sorry," she said, this time making eye contact and looking genuinely sorry. "I'll try to get home early tomorrow. We have those mushroom raviolis from Pasta Evangelists, and I can get some nice white wine on the way back from work."

He couldn't help but smile. She knew the way to his heart. "That sounds like genuine paradise."

"You know, in New York there will be none of this bullshit," he continued, sitting on the bed and easing himself into his favourite subject "I won't have clients halfway across the world. A few trips to the west coast, but all direct flights."

Her face imperceptibly dropped. "That sounds amazing," she said, looking again somewhere beyond her phone. "I can't wait."

"Oh don't worry," he said, immediately sorry he'd brought up the subject. "How is your job-hunt going? Have you heard back from Peterman's?"

She nodded, pushing her lower lip forward to form an exaggerated frown. "No dice. They're not looking for new account managers at the moment, senior or otherwise. Unless I bring in new clients." She chuckled. "As if Lewis would let me anywhere near any of those."

Her new boss, Lewis, had been a nightmare from day one. Part of her accepting the idea of moving across the Atlantic was the prospect of getting away from him.

Someone knocked on the door. It must be the food. Airport hotel room service is its own particular class of disappointment. Lord knows why they even offer it. It's probably part of their effort to make you think they are basically the Four Seasons, when they are really not.

"I need to go, babe," he said, using their ironic pet name in an unironic way.

"Go on, babe," she said, very ironically. "I miss you. Have a good night!"

And like that she was off. In the first days of their relationship, Alex had thought her a little cold. He had subsequently come to realise that she was just perennially in a hurry. That's what made her so spectacular at her job, and such a good travel partner. She got you from A to B in as expeditious a manner as humanly possible.

The burger he'd ordered was, as predicted, very depressing. Plastic bread stained with the watery juices of a rubber patty. A single slice of under-ripe tomato. He ate half of the meal, and turned on Netflix on his laptop. As he was scouring his account for something to watch, a bridal show popped up on his screen. He'd seen trailers for this one: women try on wedding dresses and their families give them very mean advice. Why was that amongst his suggestions? It could be random, or it could be that Sarah had been watching "related content". More wedding stuff. This was a problem.

He'd first found the wedding magazine while looking for his black-tie shoes in their closet. It wasn't hidden per se, but it was neatly tucked away in the corner. There were two pages folded down. Both had pictures of models that looked as much like Sarah as any model could: very thin, with swan-like necks, both brunettes. Both wearing wedding gowns, obviously. He brushed it off as an oddity. A month later, while using her Facebook account to track down the address of a party they were late for, he noticed her targeted ads. They were all baby related. Toys, baby classes, baby books. An egg-freezing service for women wanting to delay their child-rearing years. That had him thinking.

And now this. Did she want to get married, have a baby? They'd always agreed that was not for them. It was one of the things they had been relieved to agree on when they first started going out. They had met in London only three weeks after he'd moved down to start his first job in finance after university. She had also been a brand-new Londoner, in the process of getting noticed in her graduate scheme. They were both ambitious and giddy with excitement about their new adventure in the Big City. Their first dates were also many of his London firsts: first walk on Southbank, first movie at the RFI, first brunch in Shoreditch. First night-bus back to hers.

Sarah shared an ex-council flat in London Bridge with only one other girl, a mousey PhD student who rarely came out of her room. Within a few months of dating he'd all but moved in with Sarah, reluctant to return every night to his own awkward and uncomfortable house-share in Tooting Bec. When Sarah's flatmate moved on to greener pastures, it made sense for him to move in. It was only a year into their relationship, and eyebrows were raised by friends on both sides of the aisle. Alex and Sarah didn't care.

They were happy, and confident their happiness was enough. They both worked so hard over the following fourteen years that living together was the only way to see each other during the week. They shared all-nighters, stressful meetings and bullying bosses. They shared many promotions, plenty of job changes and many dreams for the future. Finally, they bought their first home together, a very tiny and very modern flat in Canary Wharf virtually across the street from Alex's job. It was a place meant for two, because they always intended to remain a family of two.

While Sarah loved her nieces, she could never see herself as a mother and said so with a level of confidence that Alex found very attractive. They had built their lives around the idea that their hearts were full with just the two of them. People had recently started to notice. After they both turned thirty-five, comments dripped in from family and friends. When's the wedding? Do you two not want children? Alex would make such a fantastic dad. Sarah would be such a lovely mum. And those comments made him think. Did she want children? Did he?

Everything would be better in New York. If he could only get them to New York. As he lay in bed, in the complete darkness of his hotel room only punctuated by the red glare of the digital alarm clock, Alex could not help but smile at the thought of the move. It had taken him years, but he had finally secured a transfer to the New York office. The Mecca of personal wealth management, where careers are made. Senior partners in the office, people he looked up to and admired, often talked about their New York days with a sense of fondness. He would even retain his biggest client, an American who split his time between Boston and London and who had been thrilled to hear he was moving to the East Coast. It would be good for Sarah too. For a marketing executive, New York was the place to be. She had been stuck under a boss who did not appreciate her, and had seriously itchy feet. What had started off as a great opportunity was now slowly strangling her career; moving to New York was the perfect way to get out. And Alex was willing to bet that once she was again in a job she loved, with a whole new continent to explore, Sarah would forget all about wedding dresses and babies. Hopefully.

The following morning he got up at an eye-watering time (his mother used to say there should only be one four o'clock in the day). He got onto his horrible cheap flight and landed at one of London's more horrible and cheaper airports. Quite a contrast from his original plan of landing at City Airport in business class, but he had to get home. He sat on a very long and nausea inducing journey, working on his laptop to catch up on the day that was already getting away from him.

Once the black cab pulled up in front of his building in Canary Wharf, it was past eleven. He'd not had breakfast, and was feeling decidedly queasy and faint. He weakly waved to the doorman as he made his way to the elevator. He finally wobbled into his tiny apartment. The overwhelming relief of home washed over his shoulders like a hot shower. While many people would have thought of Alex and Sarah's flat as cold or impersonal, to them it stood as a sweet oasis of quiet in their very complicated and busy lives. Simple lines, minimalist decor and exceptional views over the canal. A white kitchen with shiny white countertops, leading to an open-space living area entirely surrounded by floor-to-ceiling windows. Paradise.

On the kitchen island, Sarah had left him a brown paper bag. Two cheese and ham croissants. They were fresh, she must have picked them up for him on her morning run. She had also, movingly, cleaned out his Italian espresso cup and placed it in the Nespresso machine, a fresh Ristretto capsule already loaded. Her mornings were hectic, she must have moved up her alarm clock just for him.

As the Nespresso rumbled and spluttered, he collapsed in his favourite spot: a leather reading chair in the corner, surrounded by windows on all sides. He watched the usual procession of well-dressed men and women scurrying around on the pavement. His chair was angled so you could catch a perspective all the way up the canal, a thin corridor of water between tall walls of glass that opened up in the bright space of the River Thames. In the evenings, he would sit there and take a minute to enjoy looking at the lights, slowly going off one by one as workers packed up and went home. Most of the people who worked in the surrounding buildings took a train every night. He loved being able to just stroll across the tiny pedestrian bridge and run upstairs, in his pyjamas before most of his colleagues had even made it onto the train. He loved living there.

"We don't actually have to sell this flat, do we?" he asked Sarah that evening.

She'd come home earlier than usual, brandishing a bottle of white wine as promised. She'd missed him, and did not mind playing hooky from her late meeting to have dinner together. They were perched on the stools at their kitchen island, which doubled as a dining table, swilling the white wine after hoovering up their posh pasta dinner.

"What do you mean?" Her eyes were glassy with tiredness and alcohol.

"We could just rent it out, I suppose. Have it for when we come back after New York."

She angled her head slightly, as she did when she really considered a problem. "Well," she said slowly. "Is this the type of place we'll want, in eight or ten years' time?"

That sentence caught him off-guard. That was exactly the sort of place he thought he would want in eight or ten years. But he loved Sarah so much, and could not bear to see her unhappy. And he'd had too much wine. He waved his hand around in a grandiose gesture. "Maybe not. Maybe we'll need something with more space, and a big garden." Why had he said that? The thought of a big garden, and for that matter anything that would require a big garden, filled him with dread. But he loved her so much.

"And selling will free up some cash to get us a really nice place in New York. It would be so great if we could live downtown. Avoid taking the subway."

"I guess that depends on where your job will be," he continued, grateful for the opportunity to change the subject.

Her face dropped. Her voice filled with genuine sadness. For one of London's finest young marketing executives, she had a devastating lack of self-confidence. "I hope I'll get something."

"Of course you will!"

"What if I don't?"

"You will. You know it."

"But what if I didn't? Finding someone to sponsor a visa is so difficult, especially nowadays."

"It will be all right."

"Alex," she said, and he could tell she was serious. She looked straight into his eyes, without blinking. She suddenly looked sober. "If I do not get a job, how are we going to stay together?"

He had genuinely not thought about that possibility. For a fleeting second, he felt like a fool. "You will." He was aware he sounded hollow. "And if you don't, we will be long distance for a while until you do. We've been together for fifteen years, I think we can be apart for a few months."

She looked sad. "Fair enough," she said quietly. Had she wanted him to propose? While he acted aloof, Alex was very aware of the fact that if they did get married, Sarah could come with him to America and figure out jobs from there. Which would be easier. Plenty of their friends had gone through with "visa marriages": couples who would otherwise be quite happy remaining unmarried who signed the paperwork to make international moves easier. A lot of those after Brexit of course. Their friends Tobias and Marie had recently held a small dinner to celebrate their own, entirely aimed at securing Marie's future in this country. Is that what Sarah was driving at?

"I'll call the estate agent then," she continued, pouring herself the remainder of the wine bottle. "We don't have much time before you leave."

5

PAUL
MISUNDERSTANDINGS

Getting back on the property market, for real this time, had been more complicated than originally anticipated. First of all, his budget had been slashed. While most of the deposit he and Alice were planning on using came from his side of the family, he was eligible for a far smaller mortgage as a single man than he was when he was in a couple. The smaller budget meant all the houses he'd earmarked years ago were now out of his reach. He had to regroup, pivot. Find something else that excited him. Instead of semi-detached houses and flats in trendy areas of town, Paul could now afford small flats in the less exciting parts of London. Nothing grotty, just not what he'd envisaged.

This led to his second problem. While all the houses he was eyeing when he was with Alice easily lent themselves to be converted as family homes, all the places he was currently looking at were decidedly dwellings for one, maybe two, people. This had further crystallised in his mind the unpalatable fact he had tried to sugar-coat for himself for the last two years. The life he thought he would have had had been cancelled. He was not going to get married young, have children in his late twenties and live a life of bliss with his blonde, athletic, intelligent wife. His twenties were almost over for a start. He probably still would get married and have a family, his counsellor had helped him recognise, just not the way he'd imagined. And his wife would probably be intelligent, but she might not be athletic, or blonde.

The third problem for Paul, and for the rest of the country, was that the real estate market was nonsensical. He had to deal with estate agents who seemed to perversely enjoy provoking him with a series of increasingly twattish ties; he had to deal with ridiculous prices and the knowledge that he only had a handful of days to make an offer on a property before it was gone. Not ideal for someone recovering from a nervous breakdown.

The fourth problem, unique to Paul this time, was that he had started dating again. Properly. He'd been sitting in his parents' house in Kent on a Saturday morning, looking forward to a roast lunch, when he'd realised he was ready. A girl had come over to take measurements for his mother's new curtains, and he'd felt an unmistakeable twinge of excitement. She was hot. She was funny. She had a master's degree in English Literature from Warwick and was currently saving up for a PhD. He'd held the ladder steady for her as she climbed up, and her flowing skirt had brushed up against his arm. He'd wanted to go on a date with her. She'd had a boyfriend. The boyfriend, however, was immaterial. It wasn't so much about the curtains girl, it was the fact he was capable of wanting to ask someone out.

Back in London, he'd decided to take the plunge. He'd re-joined the dating apps he had used for meaningless hook-ups in the wake of Alice leaving, and started looking for someone to go out on a date with. So far so good. The problem was, London seemed devoid of any women aged twenty-eight to thirty-two who both found him attractive enough to swipe on his face and were not completely unhinged. Not unhinged in the sense of having mental health struggles: Paul would not have minded and may even have preferred having someone who could relate to his own issues. These women ranged from the hopelessly weird to the very odd indeed, with a whole spectrum of racist, shallow and plain boring in the middle. The Undateables, Croydon edition.

Of course, he was not limiting himself to dating apps. He was going to night classes that might entice women: salsa dancing, pottery, French. Things he had no interest in: he hated dancing, disliked having clay on his hands, and was already so fluent in French he had to make mistakes on purpose to fit in at the course. No dice. Every female there was married, gay or fifty. Maybe all the women looking for men were taking woodwork, football and beer brewing in the hope to run into eligible bachelors. He was also going to parties, but the issue with his friends both old and new is that after a while he got to know all of their friends too. Essentially, as he explained to his mother during their Sunday afternoon calls, there were no dateable women in London.

He was fortunate, however, in that he had plenty of women in his life to help him out with the house-hunt. Most of his publishing friends were female, and they all enjoyed taking turns to come with him to viewings and scouting potential neighbourhoods. While not particularly into old-school gender roles, Paul had to admit the women in his life saw the world differently from how he did. They spotted things he would not otherwise notice. One flat looked perfectly fine to him until he went back for a second viewing with a friend, who pointed out that all the bedrooms were south-facing and would be roasting in the summer, as well as being inundated with light before 5am. Another one had enticed him with authentic period 1920s features to the point he had neglected to notice that it was on the other side of the road from a very famous and constantly full pub. Not what you want when you head home after a long day at the office, or if you want to work from home.

Holly, the tall girl with the dyed hair who had once kissed him at a bus stop, was especially useful. More than useful, she was fun. They'd taken to roaming the streets near a potential viewing, on the lookout for crack-houses or promising bistros. Her presence helped him not look like a dangerous stalker as he checked out the front door of the house in question before phoning the agent to ask for a viewing. Holly struck up conversations with neighbours and extracted useful information about the dampness of the basements and the laziness of the freeholders. Useful. And fun.

Unfortunately, on that specific evening she had not been able to come. She had a big project due in a couple of days, and could not take the afternoon off work. So Paul was on his own, roaming the streets of South London on his way to a viewing. He'd taken the whole morning off and walked from Crystal Palace for no other reason than he liked the architecture of the station. He'd found a newsagent with mint Cornettos, and was methodically eating the chocolate bottom of his cone while keeping an eye on the map on his phone. All in all, he was in a good mood.

He found the street, and immediately spotted the house. It was difficult to do otherwise: it was a faded shade of pink, like the delicate inside of a seashell. In the late-May sunshine, the wisteria out front was covered in delicate purple blooms, almost like a swarm of microscopic butterflies. What was this tiny slice of romance doing in this drab, depressing row of clean but otherwise unremarkable 1950 terraces?

The door was white, and open. A woman was standing in the doorway, wearing a nautical-style striped shirt stretched over her pregnant belly. She had on bright red trousers and no shoes.

She had a whole mess of long blonde hair, slightly wavy and streaked by the sun. As he approached, she waved.

"Are you Paul?" she asked in a soft posh voice.

"That's right."

"Nice to meet you," she said, stepping on the front steps with her bare feet to shake his hand. "I'm Florence. I'm really sorry, but the estate agent just called me to cancel. I thought *I* could show you around though, if you don't mind."

"Oh, that's fine." *Oh no*, he thought. Are we going to have to make conversation?

His concern was immediately alleviated by a loud barking. A large dog, with long, shiny and inexplicably shaggy hair, came bounding from the inside. His tail was waving frantically as he sniffed Paul's crotch.

"Spencer!" Florence called. "Spencer, no! Spencer, down!" She giggled. Spencer the dog was unstoppable. "I'm sorry," she said to Paul with an easy charm. "Our dog has absolutely no manners."

"That's okay." Paul scruffed the dog's ears as he rubbed him hard on the top of his head. It really was. Paul loved dogs.

"Please, come in. Leave your shoes on. In this mess, you'll need them."

He was slightly alarmed, and relieved, to find the mess she was referring to was a maze of green and yellow building blocks strewn around the narrow hallway. A small blond child was sitting in the middle of the blocks, carefully chewing on one.

"Tim, say hello," exhorted his mother. Tim flopped over and hid his face away in the crook of his elbow. Paul could see a cheeky smile peering through. Florence walked over and picked him up with surprising ease considering her skinny arms. "I'm sorry," she continued, moving a lock of her beachy hair away from her son's face, smiling tenderly. "We run a bit of a mad

43

house. Come through," she said, opening the door into the kitchen.

Paul loved the house. Not quite true. He liked the house, it had beautiful period features but it was a bit girly, with floral tiles in the fireplace, copper handles and light-blue cabinets in the kitchen. It was probably her place before her husband moved in, Paul reckoned. What he loved was the atmosphere.

Florence, smiling and soft spoken, giving him a tour of the little quirks of the house. Her rounded tummy, bumping into corners and furniture like a little person already. Young Tim, playing with an assortment of dinosaurs in a corner. His father, John, who shook his hand with a big grin before returning to arranging the toppings of a couple of pizzas. From the way they looked at each other, Paul could see they were truly happy. Their small blond angel, and another on the way. A gorgeous little house, which they were now trading for more space. The one bedroom and one box room would no longer work with two sets of little feet pitter-patting.

For the first time in his house search, Paul was smiling while walking away. It would need a little TLC: repaint the kitchen cabinets, change the tiles, maybe give the place an update with some interesting wallpaper, or a faux-brick wall. But for the first time since the semi-detached house with the apple trees, he could truly see himself living somewhere. It was small, a house for one or maybe two people, but it could accommodate more. It was filled with happiness: the toddler playing in the background, the parents gently going about their business. He could imagine them preparing dinner together, talking about their day, playing with their child. The husband resting his hand gently on his wife's swollen belly, feeling his baby kick.

After the child had gone to bed they would sit on the love seat in the snug, him with a glass of wine, her with a lemonade, and talk about how excited they were about their new house.

Maybe she was already making plans to do it up, make it look just right for them. Maybe she was showing him paint swatches and tile samples she'd collected during the day, and would run her hand through his hair with a quiet smile as he tried to tell the difference between shades of cream paint. They were so happy in their little pink house.

He was so euphoric about the place, and was truly heartbroken when Holly didn't like it. She pointed out it was very small and many of its quirks could easily become annoying.

"What are you going to do with that tiny conservatory?" she asked after they'd had a second viewing, walking back to the station.

"It could be my home office." Paul imagined himself editing away, surrounded by his garden.

"It's got no insulation. You'll freeze in the winter and roast in the summer. And the snug is far too small – there's barely enough room for two!"

"I could knock it through to make the whole thing open space," he replied, already envisaging it.

"I thought it was already at the top of your budget." She was right. He was silent for a while.

"Look," she said, as they got to the station. "I'm really sorry. You clearly love it, and it's really none of my business."

"No it's fine!" he said quickly. It wasn't fine.

"I just think you can do better, but a house is an emotional purchase. If you love it, if you get the feeling," she said while making imaginary quotation marks in the air, "then that's the right choice for you. You can always get rid of the conservatory and save up to make it all open-plan."

She was right. It was a long-term purchase, he didn't have to have everything right within a month. He could make it work. He got his phone out and called the agent. He wanted a third viewing. See the house, and the family, again. Then he let Holly buy him a beer at the funny-shaped pub next to the station, because she felt badly she'd been so blunt about his home. One beer turned into two, and about three bowls of those bright orange spicy prawn crackers they sold in fancy pubs. On the way back, on the long train ride, she fell asleep resting her head on his shoulder.

❧

He returned for a third viewing during his lunch break. He'd taken the afternoon off for the viewing and to go on a second date he was not at all excited about with a doctor who was on nights and had the daytime free. He was not really interested in more medical romance, and he did not particularly fancy the woman, but she'd asked him and he was too awkward to say no. In between now and getting married, he had to get around to telling her she was really nice but he just wasn't interested.

The house looked even better than it had on the first and second viewing. By all objective standards, it looked worse. Many of the toys that had been neatly stacked away in brightly coloured plastic bins in the lounge were spread around the floor and the stairs, scattered by the child and the dog in equal measure. The woman, whose name he'd already forgotten, was clearly wearing a flowered pyjama shirt over her maternity jeans. She looked slightly more frazzled, lost without her husband there. After she'd shown Paul around, she offered him a cup of tea and he said yes. She looked slightly shocked – how are you meant to tell which tea offers are genuine and which are pro-forma? However, once she'd poured him a very milky cup in a blue-and-white polka dot mug she looked relieved to be sitting with him at the dining table.

"Are you going to make an offer?" she asked him shyly.

Wow, lady, he thought. *Way to throw the book of convention to*

46

the wind. "Yes." Probably a bad idea, but he felt that conversation somehow did not count.

Her eyes filled with tears. "Thank you," she whispered. "We really really need to move."

He looked around and saw the place through her eyes. It was too small already, and it was probably getting worse by the day as more toys propped up. The new baby must be coming soon: while he was admittedly no expert, Paul thought she was close enough to giving birth. She had to be, she was huge.

He went home and slept on it. In the morning, he called the agent. He put in an offer, at asking price. It left him with about two thousand pounds to buy himself some furniture, move and paint the place but he didn't care. Two hours later, the agent called him at work. John and Florence – that's what her name was! – had been very pleased to accept his offer. The agent would be in touch soon with some paperwork.

Paul hung up the phone and carefully got up from his desk, trying to not look too excited. While he was positive he would soon issue a group text demanding a midweek pub night to celebrate his victory, he wanted to enjoy the moment for himself. He carefully stepped through the office and made it to the stairs. After the door closed behind him, he let himself go in a bizarre jump-and-fist-pump combo. It was graceless: the salsa lessons had failed to teach him to make his body move coherently. He slowly walked downstairs and stepped onto the street. He walked over to the corner coffee place and got himself a hot chocolate. He drank it quietly, walking back to the office through the leafy streets of North London. He should text everyone, let them know before they packed up their things and left the office for the day. Or maybe he could tell them all tomorrow, go to the pub then. Have today for himself.

He walked past Holly's cubicle, then stopped. She was listening to loud music through huge headphones, and he had to tap her on her shoulder. She turned round. He did not know what he was going to say before he said it.

"I got the house," he whispered, silently fist-pumping the air once more.

"That's amazing!" she whispered back, her voice comically low, and she spun around in her chair offering a high-five. Their hands clapped, silently.

"Do you want to go for a drink and celebrate?" What was he doing?

"Sounds excellent," she said, normal volume resumed. "Have you texted the others?"

Oh, right. The others. "Not yet," he replied quickly. "Gonna do it right now." And he whipped out his phone.

"I'm really happy for you," she said while he texted. "You deserve this, you know?"

"Ha-ha. Yes, of course I do. Commentary on the privileged middle class, I see."

"No, I'm serious. You've been through enough shit, you deserve a nice house. Even though it's pink and has Barbie's closet at the back." She smirked.

He felt bizarrely wounded, which was unreasonable. After all, she was saying a nice thing with a little joke attached, and not even that mean.

"All right." He turned round. "I'll see you at six."

6
___

JOHN

They had a buyer. Thank you, Jesus. They might even get to move before the baby came. There was literally nothing he would like more than to take Tim and Florence by the hand and walk out of their perversely tiny house. They would stand on the pavement, throw a match on the floor and set the whole terrace row ablaze. Poof, just like that, gone. Start fresh. Buy all new things. New clothes for them, new toys for Tim, new furniture that wasn't a hundred years old and creaky. Do it right this time.

In this fantasy, Florence would be enthusiastic about the whole thing. Maybe not the arson, but she would love the idea of new, clean things. A real sofa, not a bizarre love seat covered in a fabric that wasn't velvet and without hard lumps that jabbed you in the neck. A bed that didn't creak. New clothes that made her look like she had before. Not skinny, she'd not gained that much weight and anyways John was not that shallow. But full of life as she had been, sexy in her satin camisoles tucked in her high-waisted jeans.

For a few months there had been a pile of her old clothes in the conservatory, and he'd walked past them with a sigh of nostalgia every day. They were like old friends, reminders of a wife who was no more. A short houndstooth skirt that was one of her work staples, with a tight burgundy turtleneck. An emerald green silk dress she would wear out to bars, with knee-high suede black boots. Nowadays, she wore her daytime clothes at restaurants, not even bothering to change if there was a stain of baby food on her brightly coloured top.

They still went out, once a month, for what felt like government-mandated date nights that were getting more and more hollow. Tim was left with one of the grandmas while they hit some nice restaurant in central London, sat across from each other with nothing to say. It was important for your relationship to have regular date nights and reconnect, keep the romance alive without the stress of the kids. That's what everybody said, that's what everybody expected of them. It was the thing to do. It was unclear what the thing to do was if the person sat in front of you looked and sounded like your wife, but was nothing like her.

This would all pass, he knew. It was a rough patch, a stressful time in their marriage. At their fiftieth anniversary party, surrounded by their children and grandchildren, they would sneak away to the back of the marquee to have a quiet glass of champagne and this whole mess wouldn't be but a footnote in their love story. The kids would grow up, they would start going to school and Florence would have more time for herself. She would slowly find her footing again, maybe start painting or maybe make a small business out of her passion for reupholstering furniture. He would come home to find her absorbed in her projects, streaks of paint on her beautiful face, her hair barely pulled back by a scarf, grinning as she showed him her progress.

One day, they would be out for a date night at their local country pub and she would tell him how sorry she was that she'd checked out all those years earlier. He would tell her it didn't matter, because he had never stopped loving her. They would kiss by the roaring fire, and walk home through the fields to prevent a hangover. They'd make love trying not to wake the children, and have a lie-in the following morning. He'd bring her a breakfast tray in bed. It was little daydreams like these that kept John going day by day.

Moving would get them a step closer to that daydream. And it would give them enough room to not be constantly in each other's pockets, which would probably help. Plus, the new house was much more to his taste. If he were honest, he did not care too much about what his home looked like as long as it was comfortable. Their current house had never been comfortable, but when they moved in he'd been so blindly in lust, and in love, with Florence that he just did not care. Plus, it was not even nearly as bad when it was just the two of them. But even at its peak, the current house had never been the sort of place he'd choose to live. The new house, on the other hand, was exactly what he'd been hoping for. Large, with plenty of space for children, dogs and guests. Georgian, with generous rooms filled with light and a big garden that gave onto the fields of Surrey. A family home, a forever home.

The current owners, an old couple, had raised their whole family in that house and it showed. The decor was outdated, the paint on the walls faded, mottled by the stains of little hands. A load of tribal and various ethnic decor from faraway places they'd probably never even visited. Maybe gifts from their children as they travelled. Maybe bought in the garden centre down the road, you never know. John loved the house just the way it was, even though he had promised Florence she would get to modernise the space. She'd talked about knocking down some walls, painting soothing white over the rich red of the sitting room and the marigold-yellow kitchen. Nevertheless, you could tell that the house had been loved intensely by its owners. They were ancient now: the husband must have had a stroke as his speech was slurred, the wife just sat there timid and confused as the estate agent showed them around. They were probably going to a home.

Their friends, other couples with whom they shared weekend outings to the petting zoo and National Trust places, were enthusiastic about the new house. They looked at pictures, excited to see it in person as soon as they could move. We'll come visit, they said, even though John had the distinct feeling they would come a handful of times and then revert to their general unwillingness to cross the M25. Many of them would move out of London soon of their own accord, scattering themselves around the home counties like middle-class dandelion seeds. They would probably lose touch with most of them, and John didn't really mind.

He liked their friends, but they were not irreplaceable. They would make new friends in Surrey, people whose houses were just walking distance from their own. Their children would attend the same schools, Florence would be on the PTA with the other wives and he could go running with the husbands at the weekends. Maybe they would all play tennis together.

Florence, on the other hand, was absolutely devastated. Her eyes filled with tears whenever they discussed seeing their friends less, and she seemed to be hell-bent on organising get-togethers at every possible opportunity. "I'll miss them so much," she would say on their way home, with a raspy voice.

He personally thought it wouldn't be such a disaster if she got a new set of friends. None of the people they regularly saw now were from their lives before Tim: that crowd mostly hung out at night in wine bars and pubs and they had rapidly lost touch. They still saw each other occasionally, but John couldn't imagine that moving to Surrey would actually make that much of a difference. Nor was she concerned with his mates, all from work, whom he would keep seeing every day. The people she would miss were their parenting friends and while they were perfectly nice, he very much felt they were mostly her friends with attached husbands. He felt like an attached husband. The wives saw each other far more than the husbands did, meeting during the day for walks and at coffee shops. They complained a lot, mostly about how hard it was to be alone with their children all day. Florence might feel happier if she spent more time with some happier people.

The other benefit of moving was that it would get Florence further away from Corinne, which frankly couldn't come too soon. John and Corinne had been sneaking around together for over a year, even though he'd been breathlessly obsessed with her for far longer. From the first day he saw her, really, sat behind the reception desk. She noticed him too, with her mint-green eyes that peered from underneath her thick black fringe, sharp as a leopard's. She knew he was married, and never cared. She waited for him, like a predator, until he was so alone and lonely that all she had to do was stroll over and collect the pieces. She asked him out for a drink when Tim was just over four months old. John said no.

She asked him again six weeks later, and John watched himself say yes. He watched himself from above, like an out-of-body experience, as he waited for her shift to be over and walked out of the office with her, brazenly. He steered her to a crowded pub in Liverpool Street. He watched himself kiss her, his hand grabbing her bare knee like a claw, in the middle of the crowded bar area. They were less than a block away from work. Any number of acquaintances could have seen them, it was only a miracle that they didn't.

A month later they slept together for the first time, in her room in an all-French flat-share in Chalk Farm. The morning after, he tried to get her fired in a panic. He had no luck, Corinne was beloved by everyone. She was beautiful, had a classy accent and was friendly to everyone. She'd cleared out the front desk of all clutter, and every Monday she brought in elaborate floral arrangements that gave the place a sophisticated look. Unless he was willing to make up a good reason for getting rid of her, she was staying. Over time, he came to be very grateful for that.

Like all the French women in his dirty imagination, Corinne was the perfect mistress. She was a revolutionary in bed, and then lay there listening to him talk about his life. She didn't mind hearing about his marital problems with Florence, about how he was worried Tim was missing out by not going to nursery, about how Florence's mother was trying to pressure them into going on holiday with her to Crete.

Corinne rarely talked about herself. She was an interesting woman in her own regard, with interests and passions and friends she was happy to talk about but did not want to share with him. She always had time to text, in the middle of the work day or in the middle of the night. Crucially, she had no pretension to any more of his life than he was willing to give away. A couple of evenings a week, a sleepover every month or so. A handful of weekends, when he was supposed to be away at a conference.

She didn't intend on staying in the country for long. This was an adventure for her, a short British interlude before going back to France and figuring out what to do for a grown-up job. It was the ideal affair: it came with a built-in expiration date. Since they had started seeing each other, John felt like a better husband to Florence too. He'd been less angry, snapped at her less. They had even, paradoxically, had more sex as he was getting his fantasies fulfilled elsewhere and could just get on with the business of keeping the marriage alive. She probably didn't even care, as long as he kept being at her side, helped with bedtime routines and came along to family weekends. That worked fine for him. Sometimes he even imagined that she knew, that she had known all along and didn't care. Maybe she was grateful she didn't have to hold his attention anymore. Like those American polygamists on television, perhaps she felt as though she was delegating the aspects of her marriage she did not care for to someone else. Sex, dressing up to go out for dinner, listening to her husband talk about his small problems.

Of course, that couldn't be true. Florence didn't know. She could never sit there in front of him if she knew, without saying a word. Would she leave if she found out? In all honesty, probably not. They were building something, a family, and she wouldn't throw it all away just like that. At any rate, the chances of him getting caught would drop significantly now they were moving to Surrey.

Once Corinne moved back to France, in a couple of years, it would be over. He wouldn't do it again, he wouldn't fall in another honey trap. He would behave himself and be there for his wife once she came out of her funk. It was perfect timing, really. Everyone should do this, it would save so many marriages. Most successful couples probably did do this, it was just never talked about. The best-kept marriage secret: have an affair.

7

MICHAEL

It was all happening so fast. One day, they'd put the house on the market "just to see what it would fetch". Another day, people were coming in for viewings. Then they had an offer. Then they had an exchange date. The whole process over before he had even really come to terms with the fact it was going to happen. For all that he'd been trying to push Claire, Michael very much loathed the idea of selling their home. Even though he proclaimed the contrary, he even enjoyed it now it was mostly empty. He felt heartbroken at the thought of leaving.

The estate agent had been wonderful. A kind girl, she understood immediately how much it hurt for them to abandon their home. She took care of everything, walked the prospective buyers through their rooms while chattering endlessly and answering all questions. Claire just sat there, on the old wing chair in the hallway they never ever used, stroking Marmalade and watching the people walk through. Mostly couples in their early thirties, mostly with one or two children. A handful of pregnant women. They all walked around the house and often made comments that while polite went straight through Claire's heart.

"We could knock that wall through," they would say, pointing at the wall between the kitchen and the dining room. "Maybe even that one," they would add, pointing at the wall between the dining room and the living room. "Make it open space." What was it with today's youth and open-space living? Jacob's house in Streatham was, or rather they had gutted it to make it so, turning all the rooms into one room, which somehow looked smaller and messier than all the original spaces put together. They loved it. Ah, every generation has its own stupid thing it does. That and kitchen islands. "We could put an island here," had said the woman who was actually buying the house, standing right at the edge of the dining room.

"Florence, there's no room to get around," the husband replied, a large red-faced man with enormous shoulders and a terrible Oxford shirt that made him look even broader and, somehow, redder.

"There will be if you knock down the wall," Michael had said, but they did not seem to understand him. Claire was pretending to read a magazine and refused to translate. They smiled, kindly, and moved on to dissect everything that was wrong with the utility room. Michael was used to his speech being an obstacle. It had started deteriorating in the late nineties, a delayed consequence of his brain injury. Just as he'd gotten used to the cane and the limping, down came the slurring and stuttering. Normally, he did not mind. After they stopped travelling in the mid-naughties, he'd kept working and the speech impediment had never stopped him from doing anything he wanted to. He worked mostly from home, and conducted all of his business by email and direct message. At conferences, Claire would come with him and translate. He'd even given a speech at Elijah's wedding, with the help of the other groom's father who'd read his hilarious jokes from flashcards.

But this time, for some reason, it really bothered him. How dare they not understand him as they came into his home and rearranged it as though it belonged to them already? "There will be room for an island if you knock down the wall," he repeated, loudly and probably even less clearly. He realised he was almost shouting. The estate agent poked her head through, alarmed. She probably thought he was inches away from snapping, poor thing. The couple didn't even acknowledge him. Young people are so cruel, with their superficial kindness. He'd been disappointed when they'd made an offer. Especially since it was an offer they could not refuse. Full asking price.

"In this economy," the estate agent had said, "I would take the money and run. Houses like yours don't sell well at the moment." He could see the frustration in her eyes. She wanted them to accept the offer and get her commission. No above-asking offers were coming. Probably fair enough. Their kitchen and boiler were the same from the eighties, when they'd moved in. The last time they'd done anything to the exterior of the house was in the nineties, and it very much showed.

They'd come back for a second visit, together, asking about schools and local nightlife. Then, a week later, the estate agent called. She sounded embarrassed. They wanted a third viewing. How odd. What else was there to look at? Also, they'd already made an offer. Were they changing their mind? In fact, only the woman showed up. She waddled in, pregnant, probably just entering the third trimester.

Claire had been out to the shops, so Michael had let her in himself. He'd brandished a pen and paper he used when he had to communicate with strangers and didn't want to go through the whole rigmarole of repeating himself and pointing at things. She'd walked around quickly, not seeming very interested in any of the rooms. She'd asked to see the garden. He'd walked her out and they'd stood under a great big cloud of lilac flowers, admiring the view over the fields. They were Claire's favourite flower: a fluffy symphony of pinks, purples and whites. She liked to open her bedroom window and breathe in their scent. He wrote this all out to her, and she looked surprised.

He wrote out a second message. "The back gate to the garden gives onto a path that connects with the local public footpath," he'd scribbled. "Excellent walks!!!" Her eyes filled with tears. Oh Lord, what had he said? With four boys and one very even-headed wife, Michael was always worrying about making women cry.

"Have you been happy here?" she'd asked, looking way past him, at the tops of the trees waving in the breeze.

"Very," he'd said, without writing it down. She'd known what he'd meant.

"How long have you been married?" she'd continued. Surely, this was not a normal third viewing.

"Forty-three." He'd written on the pad.

"That's a long time." She'd sighed. As a father, Michael had felt an instinctive impulse to give her a hug. She'd looked so lost. She was probably just hormonal, he'd thought, going through the pregnancy sadness. Claire had been inconsolable with all of her pregnancies, sobbing at anything from TV advertisements to nursery rhymes. When she was pregnant with Aaron, he had brought home some baked beans for dinner and she'd cried because they were so good.

The woman had left as quickly as she'd arrived. He hadn't mentioned anything about that strange meeting to Claire. She had barely even asked about it: she had other fish to fry. Literally. Aaron and Penelope were coming home. Jacob, Elijah and Gideon were all coming down for a welcome back party. Claire was in her element, organising food, drinks and decorations. They were coming back from Yemen, he tried to tell her they would not care if the crabs on the barbeque were whole or just claws. She shushed him: her last boy was coming home. The whole family back together, in Surrey, for what was probably the last time given everyone's schedules. She was going to throw the best damn party of her life, or die trying. Her determination made him a little sad. There would be no room for the whole family to stay over in the new place. The new hub for family events would probably be Jacob's.

"That's the whole point, love," she said as he helped her unload the car of the last few party-planning items. "It's their time now. All we need to do is go along and try to be helpful."

"I know," he said, limping into the kitchen with a paper bag full of croissants. "What are these for?"

"Breakfasts," she replied quickly. "Nobody is going to be in the mood for a cooked breakfast the day before, are they?"

"Did you get the cherry yoghurt?" he asked. Aaron and Penelope were staying with them for a couple of weeks as they finalised their arrangements. Claire, typically thoughtful, had asked what they would like to find in the house, what they'd missed the most from home. For Aaron, it was prawn cocktail crisps. For Penelope, it was cherry yoghurt. Bless her.

"Of course I did." Claire lifted up an armful of cherry yoghurts. Three different kinds. Also plain, and a separate cherry compote, because you never know.

He leaned over his cane, dangerously, and kissed her softly on her head. "I love you," he said.

"I love you too," she replied, returning to the unpacking. "Now get to it. Elijah will be here in an hour."

Late at night, Michael, Aaron and Elijah sat in the living room by the fireplace. Claire, Penelope and Elijah's husband, Tom, had all gone to bed, as had Elijah and Tom's son, Lukas. Father and sons sat up, drinking brandy and watching the fire. The party was the following day. They needed some time to catch up. As the middle children, Elijah and Aaron always shared a special bond.

"Dad, it's really nice. Posh too." Aaron was looking at pictures of their new flat. Tiny, filled with glass and light.

"Obviously the furniture in there is ghastly now," said Elijah, who had come with them for the second viewing. "But you could really do something with the place. Give it a more homey feel."

"I just didn't think Canary Wharf was your speed," Aaron said, still surprised.

"It didn't even exist in its current form the last time your mother and I lived in London. We thought we would get a fresh start." Away from their bad memories of the place, and from anything that might make them miss Surrey. Going for a totally new vibe.

"And it has an elevator," Elijah said. Michael realised he was referencing a previous conversation he must have had with his brother. The idea of his children worrying about him, discussing his health over the phone felt foreign to him. It felt like a few months since he was fussing over his own parents, trying to get them to act their age.

"So you've found a job at King's then?" asked Elijah, shifting the conversation to employment.

"Penelope has and they've offered me a place too," replied Aaron morosely.

"I thought you'd be happy," said Michael, with no need for a pad and paper. His children understood him without fail.

"I am happy, really. It's just not what I imagined I would be doing." MSF had offered him an office job, but Aaron loved the thrill of helping people hands-on. And he was more than qualified to work in emergency medicine.

"You'll be the only one of us to actually work in a hospital," chimed in Elijah. He was a GP, Jacob was exclusively doing research at UCL after a few years spent trying to balance science with his clinical career. Gideon, of course, had been a journalist for longer than he'd ever been a doctor.

"Yippee," Aaron whispered slowly, staring into the fire.

"All right," Michael said. "What would you like to do instead?" Would parenting never end?

"Well..." Aaron's face lit up, licked by the golden light of the fire. "There is something." He leaned forward as he spoke, a glow of excitement spreading over his face. "Penelope has a friend who has been looking to set up a space for unaccompanied minors, children who have come through hell to get to the UK and have nobody. A refuge. Many of them are still recovering physically, so they need medical supervision, but it's mostly about teaching them to settle in, helping them heal."

"That's amazing!" Elijah chimed in. "Why aren't you doing that, instead?"

"It's more of a pipe dream than anything else. Penelope helped her friend get an application for funding together, but the way the system works means we are unlikely to get funding unless we already have a space set up."

"What?"

"Yeah, it's really fucked up. They only support initiatives that are stable." He made quotation marks with his fingers, frowning with disgust. "And that means that unless you already have an established place and at least some staff on board, you're never getting through the first stage of triage."

"That's awful."

"I know. This government, man."

Michael couldn't help but smile. His children were so much like him, he could see himself in them more and more every year.

"How much would that cost?" Claire appeared in the door. She was in her pyjamas, holding a glass of cold water.

"Oh, Mum. It's not the sort of thing you could just... it's a lot of money." Aaron was embarrassed. His mother could never stop solving problems.

"Why not?" She came over and sat on Michael's armrest. She turned round to talk to him. "Our new house is quite a lot cheaper than our current house. We have money left over."

She wasn't wrong. Of course, all the boys would have to agree. It would all be theirs, one day, and Michael didn't want to go around spending their inheritance without regard for their futures. But if they agreed, and they probably would, then why not? They were getting a fresh start, why not give one to the kids?

The morning after the party, Claire took Jacob, Aaron, Elijah and Gideon for a brisk country walk. As they got back through the gate, he could see her face: she was beaming. There were actual tears in Aaron's eyes, and his brothers were taking turns wrapping their arms around him. Then they took him and Penelope out for a nice dinner at the Horse and Groom and told her. She actually cried, big tears rolling down her cheeks. Four hundred thousand pounds, enough to get a starter space. They could make such a difference, she told them in a cracked voice. There were so many kids waiting for a chance like this. And just like that, it was settled.

And then, in another flurry of important things happening too quickly for him to keep track, it all became reality. Aaron politely declined his A&E job. Penelope would take hers and was actually looking forward to it. They found a property, a four-bedroom near Gatwick: slightly run-down, but with a lot of potential. They put in an offer, a little below asking price, and it got accepted. There was someone else offering more, but the vendors were moved by their cause. Sometimes it paid off to have faith in humanity.

Claire called her old publisher and over the course of a ten-minute phone call she sold him a book of short stories collected from the first intake of children. The proceeds would go straight back to the refuge, help expand it. Aaron filed their application for government funds and heard back in record time; they were in business. Terrifyingly, a list of children appeared, and a date for them to move into the refuge.

"It's going to be a tight turnaround," Aaron said, standing in the kitchen of their Surrey home. The timeline of events was scribbled in colourful marker over a large piece of paper taped to the refrigerator, like when they were kids.

"You exchange on the 31st." He pointed at the chart. "Hopefully complete on the 10th. We'll then exchange and complete on the same day, on the 13th. We'll move in on the 13th and get to work cleaning up the place, which gives us barely enough time before the children move in, on the 29th."

"That *is* tight," said Michael, "but we've been through worse, haven't we?" They had. Aaron had sat his GCSEs three hours after they had landed back in the UK after a nine-month assignment in Madagascar. Jacob and Gideon had once relied on a twenty-five minute airplane connection across terminals to make it to Aaron's wedding. They were a family that planned for success.

"The main problem could be not getting the refuge ready in time." Penelope slipped on her trainers. She was commuting every day into London, driving to Denmark Hill for her job. It was exhausting, but it would get easier once they moved closer to the city.

"I spoke to some of the staff we've already recruited and they said they would not mind helping out," Aaron replied.

"Who have you hired?" Michael felt as though he was in the way of the husband and wife team working together: they both knew the ins and outs of the refuge, he felt like he was always playing catch up.

"A couple of residential staff, and a psychologist and a nurse who can go in twice a week. Really nice people." Aaron frowned. "I'd just like for the whole hiring process to be easier." After years living in precarious conditions, the shackles of bureaucracy seemed to overwhelm him.

"The residential women both worked at a posh public school before." Penelope put on her hoodie as she opened the door. "I don't know how long they'll last."

"It will be all right," Aaron said curtly. "We'll be there to help."

Penelope left quickly. Michael felt that particular discussion had been had many times.

"This is harder to do with only civilians," Aaron said quietly. "I'm afraid I am somewhat out of touch."

"I know how you feel." Michael put his hand on his son's shoulder. "You'll settle back into England before you know it. You just need this whole project to kick off, and you'll feel right at home."

8

SARAH

They were exchanging on the 31st. That left them sixteen days, including weekends, to complete, pack up and make it over to New York before Alex's first day at work. Any delays, and she would stay, joining him once everything was settled. If she joined him at all. The question was weighing on her mind. With no job to speak of in sight, it was getting more and more unlikely she would be able to start straight away. According to their original plan, they would leave in less than a month. If nothing else, at this point she had to hand in her notice at work within the next couple of days if she intended to actually leave with Alex. That, however, was not the issue. Did she even want to go? She certainly wanted to move to New York. She just wasn't sure whether she wanted to go with Alex.

It had all started with his unwillingness to admit that she may not find a job. She was getting relatively senior, and jobs at that level were few and far between. While she had no doubt she could land one within the space of a year or so, doing so within a few months was always going to be difficult. The obvious thing to do, from Sarah's perspective, was to quickly get married, go over together and she could keep applying for jobs from over there. This would make the search easier, as she could network, invite people over for coffee and generally make a better impression. They had savings and Alex would earn plenty of money. They did not need her to start work straight away. She sort of assumed this was implied, but the more hints she dropped the more he made it clear he heard her, and disagreed. The issue couldn't be the marriage. They had friends who had visa weddings all the time, and Alex had always said it was a very sensible way to get things done. Clearly, the issue was Sarah. He didn't mind getting married, but he did mind getting married to her. And she was starting to agree: where they had once agreed on everything, she couldn't help but feel they were going in two different directions in life. For one, she was almost certain he wanted kids.

At first, she thought she was being paranoid. Every time they had even vaguely talked about children, Alex had always agreed with her that it was not for them. For one, neither of them really liked babies. She quite liked children five and up, but not for long periods of time. She loved visiting her sister, but playing with her nieces was never the highlight of the trip. Sarah never seemed to click with them, she could never understand what they wanted, or what they thought was entertaining. Alex didn't even particularly like older children. He had no patience for games, and didn't really enjoy talking to them. And yet, increasingly she got the feeling there was something really important bothering him.

She'd asked him, and he'd put it down to the pressure of wanting to move. Angling for the right clients, positioning himself just right so that his request to transfer to New York would seem like a good move for the firm. She'd even believed him, for a while. But she couldn't help but wonder. Then he'd started to ask odd questions.

"Would you like to have a wedding, someday?" he asked

her one evening. They'd been to a posh fundraiser, and were sitting on the night-bus home. He was wearing his black-tie suit, and looked handsome, like James Bond. She thought he must have been drunk, and laughed it off. Then, when he insisted, she thought it might be a joke. She was knee-deep in wedding stuff for one of her clients, a famous gown designer. She'd even been taking some of it home, learning names of wedding dress styles and earmarking photos in magazines where they had totally gone off-brand. She hated that assignment, it was a small client who didn't bill a lot of hours. The only reason, the only possible reason it had landed on her already very busy desk was that she was a woman, and her boss, Lewis, was a sexist. Not a sexist, a dick. Sarah laughed even more, and told Alex to stop it. He'd looked troubled. Had he meant it?

He kept dropping hints over the next couple of weeks, and she became convinced he really was changing his mind about the whole marriage-and-kids situation. He even hinted that once they moved back from New York they might want to get a bigger house, with a garden. How could they be on such different pages if up until now they'd been in complete unison? She was thinking once they got back they could get an even slicker, even cooler apartment, on a higher floor of a tall building, with breathtaking views of the city at their feet. He, apparently, was thinking about detached homes with large gardens near to good schools.

At first, she perceived it as a betrayal. How dare he. They had talked about this. She remembered when, a year or so into their dating life, they'd spent a Saturday afternoon strolling around Borough Market eating goat's milk gelato and making their plans. They would both climb to the top of their professions. They would get a slick apartment. They would spend some time abroad, Berlin or New York. Experience all these cities had to offer. They would retire early and travel the world, maybe start a B&B in Costa Rica. How dare he betray all of that.

Then, she started thinking it wasn't all his fault. Her friends who had chosen to have children all talked about motherhood as though it was an unavoidable instinct. Maybe once you had it, you had it. Like a deadly virus. It was a primal call of nature, something you could not ignore. Maybe that's what was happening to Alex. She loved him so much. Would he leave her for a woman who wanted to carry his children? Was that what the New York move was all about?

That would make sense. He seemed more and more in a hurry to move, rushing through the weeks and months until, as he put it, "They made it to New York." Like New York was a haven, a place he had to reach to make it to safety. From her.

She started researching options. Could she freeze her eggs? Buy some more time, for him to change his mind or for her to pluck up the courage and do it. She spent a terrifying Sunday googling babies. It was like researching an alien species. The whole process, from getting pregnant to giving birth to getting the little snot-covered monster to eat, walk and use the bathroom properly filled her with dread. She actually got nauseous. She couldn't do it. She could never do it. What did that mean for them? More and more, Alex seemed to brush off her concerns about not finding a job. While at the beginning this had been nice, a boost of confidence knowing she had a cheerleader in him, she started to think that perhaps he didn't much care if she got a job or not.

If she didn't, he would move to New York alone. He would be free. He probably wouldn't even need to break up with her. Or maybe he wasn't even thinking that far. Maybe he just wanted to get away from her for some space. And once he made it to New York, he was bound to meet other women. Women who were younger, but just as smart and good-looking. Women who could not wait to start a family, and who would fall over themselves for a handsome, athletic, rich English man who was broody for babies. They would get a dog, a house in New Jersey from which he could commute in. They would pop out four children in six years, and live happily ever after. Fuck him. If that's what he wanted, that's what he should get.

Sarah contemplated her CV, staring back at her from her computer screen. It was the middle of the day, she should be working instead of sending off job applications to increasingly obscure US firms. This one wasn't even in New York, it was in Jersey City. With each rejection, she kept applying for jobs that were less and less suitable, and further and further away. This may be crossing a line. The whole idea of them living in Manhattan and walking to work was never going to be feasible with her commuting an hour each way by car. If that was even the idea anymore. Plus, this firm was small: their largest client was smaller than the smallest client Sarah had handled in years. She probably would get the job, she was beyond overqualified. But did she even want it? Her reputation could never recover from a job like that. Never come back to jobs like the one she had now. Sarah looked around her. She loved her work. No number of sexist bosses or stubborn clients could ever disguise how happy she was every day walking in the door.

It was a smart office, with green glass partitions and a clever carpet with different bright colours in different areas, signifying different departments. Accounting was orange, client relations bright teal. Sarah's carpet was electric blue. She liked to wear colours that popped against the carpet: mustard yellow, aqua, bright white. Today it was a fuchsia blouse, tucked into her wide-leg black crepe trousers. Her shoes were black, tall and impractical. She loved dressing up for work. At the small firm in New Jersey, people probably went in wearing jeans and a hoodie on Friday. She would stand out like a parrot in a plaza full of pigeons. She might have to buy new clothes, dumpier, sadder items to make her fit in with her new surroundings. *No*, she thought, while getting up. She was late for a client lunch. *I won't apply to this. In fact, I am done applying to things. I'm done.*

She was shocked with herself, with how quickly she made a backup plan. She was still waiting to hear from a couple of the good jobs. If nothing materialised, she would wait until Alex left and then move in with her sister. Temporarily. When she had called and asked if it was okay, Julia had been her usual, reliable self. Of course, she'd said, anything you need. She was expecting information in return. Were she and Alex breaking up? If so, why? If not, why wasn't she going with him to America? All good questions. Sarah would have to figure out the answers later. They could stay together and attempt long distance, until he inevitably left her for a younger, more fertile, broodier woman. She could leave him, and live forever a broken person, half of a whole. She could bite the bullet and just give in, have a baby. She would have all her evenings free to think, once the flat sold.

9

HOLLY
CRISIS

I
t was an unseasonably cold evening. It had been raining all day, and the garden was sodden and grey. Holly shivered underneath her blanket, a coarse tweed mammoth marred by moth-holes. She glanced upwards, towards the mould stain on the ceiling. In spite of her regularly soaking it in bleach, it was coming back. She hated that house. That wasn't strictly true, she thought, as she got up from the creaky sofa to make herself a cup of tea. That run-down cottage had gifted her with so many happy childhood memories when her granny lived there. During the summer, her mum would drop her off for a whole week, and she and Granny would get to go on long walks in the countryside, bake and make jams and chutneys. In the evening, they sat on that sofa and Granny read books to her, mostly inappropriate for her age. They had gone through the literary classics: that's where her love for literature was born. It had been magical.

However, by the time Granny died it was no longer magical. It had been severely neglected, and upkeep had essentially stopped since Granddad had died in the early nineties. The garden, once a charming cloud of well-groomed roses and herbs, was now overgrown with weeds. There was no insulation to speak of, the boiler managed to heat up enough water to shower and do dishes but heating was dependent on a smoky wood stove in the corner of the lounge. The kitchen was the worst: it had been so deeply used and deeply loved, but the white linoleum was now a pale-yellow colour and was peeling at every corner. The countertops were covered in deep brown stains, and there was rust everywhere.

Yet, Granny had left it to Holly. The only child of her only child. Her dad had offered to help her sell it, but Holly was desperate to save money and the opportunity to earn London wages while not having any living expenses was too tempting. She would move in, live there rent-free and slowly try to fix it up. Once she had saved enough money to take on her Great Round The World Adventure, she could sell it and stash the money away as a nest egg for when she came back. While the DIY renovation plan had almost immediately ground to a halt, she was saving a lot of money. On the other hand, life was pretty uncomfortable. As well as crumbling, the cottage was half-filled with her granny's possessions, things that she hadn't taken with her into the care home.

Holly had sorted through her clothes to make space in the closet: she'd donated some, but she'd mostly held on to her dead granny's dresses. They were fabulous, and vintage was back in fashion. While totally inept at most of the feminine arts of cooking and cleaning, Holly was a good enough seamstress to adapt some of those authentic vintage pieces for herself. She even had an ancient but still functioning sewing machine, occupying such a permanent spot at the kitchen table it was essentially glued to the gingham oil tablecloth that was nailed to the tabletop. On the sewing machine, Holly altered a red summer dress, cut from ankle-length to end right above her knee. She made a green velvet dress sleeveless, to wear out to bars. She turned her granny's floral pattern house dresses into blouses, to go over boyfriend jeans or with a little skirt.

Aside from the clothes, Holly hadn't touched much. There was crockery and cutlery, mostly mismatched, and an astounding collection of Tupperware containers. There were some old books, mostly detective stories and romance novels Granny had bought from mail-order catalogues decades earlier. The clutter didn't make the house uncomfortable, but it was not pleasant to rest in. Not that it mattered, Holly spent a lot of time out of the house. Mostly in London, hanging out with her friends from work. Although at this point they were hardly "friends from work" any more, they were genuine friends.

Her phone buzzed, and kept on buzzing. Not a text. Someone was calling. How strange. An uncommon enough occurrence these days, when texts seemed to cover the whole spectrum of human communication. Even more strangely, it was not her mum, it was Paul.

"Hey, pussycat," said the voice at the other end of the line.

"What?" That couldn't be Paul.

"I'm sorry, I was trying to do a joke. Having a bit of a crisis down here."

"Oh no, what's happened?" She sat down again, noticing another hole in her thick tights. Bugger.

"You know how I was supposed to move in two weeks' time?"

"Yeah." The Move. Paul had hardly talked about it. For some reason, since he'd put in an offer on his new house they had been spending less time together. Maybe he had only found her opinion useful on house viewings. No viewings, no hangouts. Fair enough.

"The move is off." His voice was slightly cracked, like he'd been at a football game.

"What?" That could not be.

"It's off. Exchange was meant to be tomorrow, and it's off. Sellers pulled out."

"It's off? Can they even do that?" Could they? God, people were assholes. She hated that she owned a house. Crappy as it was, it still made her part of the landed gentry. The term "homeowners" on a newspaper headline applied, undeniably, to her.

"They can." He sounded defeated.

"But why?"

"No idea. They don't even have to tell me why. But I think they decided to stay. They probably had too many happy memories in that house, it's where their child was born. Bet they're just doing an extension somehow to fit in their second baby."

"That's shitty." Was he drunk? Was he drunk calling her? Holly had to be careful. Once he drunk called her there was no going back. No pretending to be friends, unless they were friends, of course. "Are you drunk?" she asked.

"A little. I thought it would make me feel better but it hasn't. Now I'm drunk, and imminently homeless."

"Oh shit. I forgot. You still need to move out in two weeks, right?"

"Right. The place is already let to someone else. I have no choice, I'm out on my ass."

"What are you gonna do?" She spoke without thinking. "Do you need a place to stay?"

"Oh my God, yes." He sounded desperate.

"You do know I live in Essex, right? It's ages away, and my house is a shithole."

"Oh, I'm sorry," he sounded wounded. "Did you not actually mean it about a place to stay?"

"No no, of course I do. It's just not very guest-ready is all."

"I mean, don't worry, I can ask Chris and Lizzie if they'll have me." Their other friends from work shared a tiny one-bedroom flat and definitely didn't have any room.

"That's not what I meant. It'd be great to have you!" She smiled. It really would.

"I am so grateful, Holly. It will only be for a couple of weeks, until we get this sorted out. I really think the sellers might change their mind."

"No problem," she said. "When can you move in?"

Suddenly, she had a lodger. Because he was getting his own room, Paul had insisted on paying rent, however symbolic. The cost of a takeout for two a week. He came up on the train, and she met him halfway to help carry his things. Surprisingly very few possessions for a man of almost three decades. They walked from the station, along an overgrown path through the tall grass next to the train line, him carrying his two suitcases of clothes and her juggling a large cardboard box of books. He did look slightly shocked when he first saw the cottage. Looking at it from an outsider's perspective, Holly had to admit it was only marginally better than homelessness. Moss was growing under the roof tiles. The outside paint was saturated with soot from the chimney, and was peeling at the edges. The windows, single paned, shook every time a car went by, which was thankfully rare as they were the last house in the village.

"Wow, this is old-school," he said with a grin.

"I told you, I need the money to go travelling."

"You'll deserve it after a year living here," he said, sardonically, plopping himself on his very creaky bed. She had gone through the whole room, decluttered it of various junk and re-bleached the walls. She'd thoroughly cleaned it, going over the old faded carpet twice with the hoover, and even with some special carpet shampoo she got online. It wasn't nice, but it wasn't disgusting either.

She sat down next to him, immediately aware they were both sitting on a bed, a double bed.

"How are you feeling?" she asked. She had not expected him to cry. She vigorously rubbed his back.

"I'm sorry," he sniffled. "I am really, really sorry, look at me, actually crying."

"That's okay." She rubbed his back more gently. "Want to talk about it?"

"I guess it's not really about the house."

"No shit, Sherlock." He looked wounded. She had to learn to calibrate when she spoke to him. He got offended so easily, and would spend hours with a slight shadow on his face. He never seemed to understand when she was affectionately quipping.

"I guess it's pretty obvious." He wiped his eyes with the sleeve of his jumper. It was a quirk of his, to wipe his glasses and, as needed, his eyes with the outstretched sleeves of his coarse-knit jumpers. "I think it was about my chance at proper happiness. You know, like that's the kind of house where you get to be happy."

"I'm sorry," she said. *That's horseshit*, she thought, a house couldn't make you happy any more than a job could. Maybe for a little, but not for long, and not really. This was not, she felt, the time to bring this up. "Would you like a glass of wine?"

"Yes please," he said, with a smile. "And I've brought you some gin in my bag."

Four hours later, they were halfway through the bottle of gin, it was Hendrick's, in its dark black glass bottle that looked like it would forever be full. Holly didn't have any mixer in the house, why would she, so they were drinking it mixed with a little water and vanilla essence from the baking cupboard. It was actually delicious. She'd made chicken soup earlier that day, and they sat on the small overstuffed couch drinking gin and slurping soup as they chatted.

Holly blinked deeply. Everything was a bit blurry, her contact lenses slightly drying right on her eyeballs. Paul looked blurry too. She had a terrifying flashback to a night out. Waiting for the night-bus. She had been so embarrassed the day after, but clearly he'd been so drunk he didn't remember. It was when her hair was still dark red. Now she'd changed it, it was bright turquoise at the ends with her dark, natural roots showing for a few inches. Maybe he would like that better. She leaned over, and she kissed him. She slipped, so she missed his mouth and landed somewhere between his upper lip and his nose.

He leaped back. She felt so mortified, her cheeks flush with embarrassment.

"What are you doing?" he asked.

"I'm sorry," she said. "I just got carried away. I thought you would like my hair better now it's blue." She giggled. Christ almighty, was she giggling? What next? The pizza guy was going to come round?

He sat down, looked at her with large confused eyes. "So you remember when you tried to kiss me at the bus stop?"

She laughed. "Of course. Why do men always think women can't hold their liquor?" She giggled again, comically speaking, she was on fire.

"Why didn't you say anything? I wanted to talk to you."

"It was embarrassing, wasn't it? Men are meant to get

rejected, not women! What the hell kind of office romance are we conducting here?"

He wrapped her in his arms. Things were taking a turn some kind of way. Wait, was he smelling her hair? He certainly was. Had she washed it today? Nope. Damn.

He loosened the hug just enough to look her in the face. She took off his glasses.

"I wasn't aware we were having an office romance," he said quietly.

"It's been a secret," she replied, whispering. "Until now."

Holly woke up with the sun streaming through her open curtains. In the heat of the moment, they hadn't bothered to close them the previous night. Paul was a warm presence, right behind her. Oh shit. Paul. The sex was bad, of course it was bad, they'd both been pretty drunk and her granny's bed was not the steadiest surface at any rate. Oh, God, how was she going to cope with the embarrassment? What was she going to do? She still had to see him at work, and now the sex had been bad there was really very little chance they'd get a second go. Why did she drink the gin? You don't get drunk with your best friend, whom you hopelessly fancy. It's Life 101 stuff.

She turned round, hoping to locate something to put on as she went to shower. Paul's eyes were open, which startled her.

"Good morning," she said, aiming to sound natural.

"Good morning." He wrapped her up in his arms, held her close. "I have the world's worst hangover."

"No," she corrected him gently, "you have the world's second worst hangover. I have the world's worst."

He smiled. He looked even more naked than he already was without his glasses. Where had they got to? And wait, he did not seem particularly repulsed, or ashamed. He seemed happy instead.

"We should have a talk," he said, smiling slowly. "Is there somewhere in all of Hatfield Peverel that does coffee that isn't burnt?"

She smiled. This was going to be a good talk.

And so it was. They didn't decide anything, other than whatever had happened was very much a very good idea, and they should do it again. It was a Saturday morning, they had two days to figure it out. Even if they didn't, there was no hurry. They walked back to the cottage in the golden glow of the autumnal sun, basking in its glory as it warmed up the wet pavement. The leaves on the trees were starting to turn, and the birch near the cottage was glistening with half-golden leaves.

It would be a good day to get the watercolours out, thought Holly. She said so out loud, and to her surprise Paul asked if he could watch her paint. They picked up some sandwiches from the local offie and made it to the canal. Holly painted until well into the afternoon, while Paul read his book and looked at her work, methodically.

"I should be painting you," she said. "That's what happens in all the movies."

"That's all right," he replied straight back. "There are enough pictures of pale white men out there. Paint something beautiful, like the ducks."

Obediently, she sketched out some ducks for him on her pad. It became a fun game: he'd point at something, she'd sketch it and colour it in as quickly as possible. When they got tired of this, they packed up and started walking back towards the cottage.

"Can I make you dinner?" asked Paul, respectfully, like an old-school gentleman asking for a dance.

"I would love that." Holly was not prepared for what was to

come. Paul ran, as in literally ran, to the shops and returned with a couple of mystery bags. He then secluded himself in her horrible kitchen, only to re-emerge two hours later with a true vegetarian feast. Oven-baked French onion soup, loaded with cheese. Baked sweet potato, with home-made hummus and crunchy chickpeas. Roasted red peppers, mixed with rocket, pine nuts and crunchy slithers of pink beetroot, as a sort of autumnal salad with a honey and mustard dressing. Poached pears for dessert, which sounded boring but was actually unspeakably delicious. Her granny's table had not looked so full of joy since before she went into care.

They had a magical Saturday night, and a magical Sunday. On Monday, they went to work together. No need to stagger entrances, everybody knew Paul was crashing at her place for a couple of weeks. Ideal way to take the pressure off. Tuesday was one of her work from home days, and she attempted being domestic by making spaghetti carbonara while he was at work. It was fun, even though she hated cooking and had to phone her mother three times for emergency instructions. Wednesday night she had drinks with her non-work friends, and came home late to find Paul had gone to sleep in her bed without her. She smiled as she squeezed herself in the tiny wedge of space left.

Thursday was another work from home day, and Paul joined her. They did very little work, and put on very few clothes. They watched a movie at night, snuggled together. Paul made them hot chocolates and popcorn, just because. Friday they spent working hard making up for the time they had squandered on Thursday. Holly had a project on a young adult novel she was reading due by the evening, and didn't see Paul all day.

After work, the whole work gang went out. They went for drinks, then to a gig. Holly enjoyed turning round at random moments in the night, to catch Paul staring at her with a secret grin. She couldn't help but smile herself. The rest of the group seemed oblivious, but they probably knew everything already. Why else would two people be constantly smiling to themselves? They caught the last train just in time, and made it home in total darkness. Before she knew it, she had been happy for a whole week.

10

FLORENCE

They had gotten married at the Greenwich Observatory on 1 February 2015. It had been, quite simply, the perfect wedding. She had spent six months scouring the boutiques of London and the south east for her wedding dress, often alone, sometimes with various combinations of family and friends. Every time, it was a magical experience. People are so nice to you when they find out you are engaged and planning a wedding. They gush over the engagement ring – hers was a vintage emerald John had received from his grandma. They offer you champagne as you wait, they ask you questions about the flowers, the colour scheme. She had taken her time. She planned on her wedding being her greatest art project yet. It had even been featured in a magazine. None of her art had ever made it to a magazine.

She had settled on a deceptively simple gown in ivory satin, cut to look vintage even though it was new. It was a column dress, cut narrowly to her thin frame and softly gathered at the waist. It had a deep V-neck and it made her feel beautiful. She looked even thinner than she really was in her wedding gown, and somehow the way the waist was cut under her chest made her look bustier. She left her long blonde hair flowing down her back, and carried a small bouquet of white hellebores. As she stood on the shiny black-and-white chequered floor of the room where they'd held the ceremony, she could see how she looked in John's eyes.

Her four bridesmaids all wore pale grey tulle dresses, the matt fabric contrasting against the shiny silkiness of her own gown. Her friends had loved her for it: finally a bridesmaid dress you actually want to wear again. They had purple flowers, Lenten roses that looked almost black with acerbic green centres. She had even convinced her mother to wear light pink, for no other reason than it would look good with the rest of the wedding party. John had worn his dark grey suit, as instructed, and had been in awe of the whole event. It was a misty February afternoon, very mild for that time of year but still chilly, and they had stood on the terrace for hours having their photos taken. Her family, then his family. The wedding party. All the boys, then all the girls. Then the bride and groom. Everyone looked so good, their cheeks flush with the winter wind, standing in front of a fairy-tale view of the city clouded in little ribbons of fog.

They had been so happy. There was a large-print photo of them in the hallway, kissing. It was black and white, in a white frame. No matter how busy she was, she would always stop to look at it for a second as she rushed in and out of the house. She always remembered how she'd felt on that terrace above London, looking at her new husband as though he were the only man in the world. The cold wind wrapping her body through her paper-thin dress. Not a care in the world. As she sat on the floor, with the picture frame in her hands, Florence felt deeply surprised there were no tears rolling down her cheeks. She didn't feel sad, she didn't want to cry at all. She just felt empty, as though someone had gone through her heart, packed everything up in neat little boxes and hauled it all away. She looked at her phone. It was half-past midday, on the 31st. They would have exchanged by now. They would be on their way to the next step in their lives. But they hadn't. God, she hoped this had been the right thing to do.

She had almost done it. Up until the 29th, she had been fine. She was focusing on the new house: jobs to do, flooring to choose, samples of wallpaper to pick up. John had left her with absolute power over all the redecorating decisions. Of course. She could even imagine he was feeling bad about the affair and was letting her do whatever she wanted as a way to keep her happy. In a way, she *was* happy. She picked a William Morris wallpaper for the hallway, a delicate pattern of willow leaves twirling on the wall to greet visitors to her home. They were going open space, of course, and she'd been thrilled to keep the vintage Aga that was already in there. She'd chosen a muted green for the kitchen cabinets, with wooden countertops and matt white tiles on the backsplash. She was certain John disliked it, but he hadn't dared say a word. She was playing a little game with herself. She was picking things increasingly to her taste, things she knew John would hate. She was daring him to say something. The less he protested, the more she escalated the situation. Turning the wood-panelled study into a playroom, with brightly coloured walls: silence. Pale-pink wallpaper in the master bedroom, with an embossed design of gold-leaf flowers: not a word. Come on.

And then he'd snapped. Strangely, it was over something Florence would not have imagined he would care about. *Goes to show*, she thought, *how I don't know you anymore, John*. Bathroom tiles. She'd wanted duck egg. She hadn't even considered he might not like it: it was the colour of their bathroom now and he had never commented on it. So she went ahead and just ordered the damn tiles. By the time they came, they would have already moved in. They were on sale.

He was upset. She should have checked with him first, he said, it was his house too. She should be more considerate. She should respect his feelings. That's when she lost it. Their screaming match lasted hours: the dog was initially alarmed and joined in with his barking, but eventually resigned himself and went to lie down. Tim kept watching episodes of Peppa Pig on his iPad for one, two, three hours. More screen time than he should have in a month.

John had not left quietly. Florence had imagined he may just excuse himself to pack a bag, and then quietly walk out of her life, never to be seen ever again. He was unprepared for this scenario. In fact, he looked confused that she was even bringing this up. "I thought you knew," he'd said. "Thought you wouldn't care. We've been so distant, like ships in the night."

That only made her angrier. Those were her complaints, not his. She'd not been distant, she'd poured her heart and soul into their child. He was supposed to be a man, he was supposed to get on with it. Why did he need attention, like a toddler himself?

"Everybody needs attention," he came straight back at her. "You're my wife. You're supposed to be interested in me."

"Well," she'd replied, pounding her thin fist on the hallway table, "I don't anymore. I barely even recognise you."

After begging, crying and whining, John turned and started threatening her. "You can't live without me," he'd said.

"I already am," she'd replied, coolly, and he looked as though she'd struck him in the face with a lead pipe.

"You can't move to the new house without me," he'd said.

"I don't care," she'd replied.

That he would even think she would put up with the betrayal and the humiliation of him having not an affair, but a regular mistress, for the sake of a house was absurd. His tune changed immediately. She could still move, he said, pleading. He would support her and Tim as they got out of this horrible little house. He could come visit. Maybe, with time, they could find each other again. They would heal together.

She got angry. This wasn't a horrible little house, it was a home that she had loved. That she still loved, come to think of it. Yes it was cramped, but there would be far more room without his stuff in the way. And come to think of it, she had never wanted to move out of London. London was her life, where she'd grown up. Where all of her friends were. Her friends who would get her through this, no doubt.

"They are not really your friends," he said. "They are just there out of proximity. You could find people like that anywhere."

She asked him to name two of her friends. He couldn't. He asked her to name two of his friends. She named five.

"What can I do?" he asked in a last ditch attempt. "What will get us through this. Tell me, and I will do it." That's when she started feeling empty. She didn't want anything. There was nothing that could make her forget. Now she'd spoken up, there was no way to have those words unspoken. There was nothing he could do; now those feelings had been unpacked, they would never fit again in the packaging.

"Please get out," she'd said, quietly. She didn't want to shout anymore. The tears were burning at the back of her throat, but she didn't have any more to cry.

"Why should I leave? If you want to leave, you get out!" he yelled back.

"Are you serious?" she asked, even more quietly.

"I guess not," he said then left.

They'd called off the exchange. The estate agent on the other end of the line sounded like he was about to blow a gasket, but kept his cool. Please get in touch as soon as you can if you change your mind. That's what John said too. She hadn't told her parents yet. She would need to, and soon, but couldn't cope with the overwhelming amount of things to do. She had somehow assumed that once they were separated, everything would become easier. She would be less burdened, less overwhelmed. John hadn't contributed much to the childcare, the cooking or the cleaning; she wouldn't have more on her plate. Except she had to find a lawyer. They had to figure out financial support, and visitation.

Tim, gratifyingly, seemed oblivious to all this. It was not uncommon for him to go a whole week without seeing his father, who left before he rose and often came back after he'd gone to bed. A few times a month John even stayed in the office overnight, finishing up urgent client work. *Oh shit*, she thought. He was definitely just with her, wasn't he? She had not yet connected the dots in her mind: her husband's devotion to his work had merely been dedication to his mistress. Also, this explained why it had taken him such a long time to become a partner at the firm. He had been the last of his intake to make it, and at the celebration dinner there had been many jokes from his colleagues about him joshing off at any possible opportunity. If he'd been as dedicated as she thought, there was no explaining those. At any rate, Tim was all right.

Spencer the dog, on the other hand, seemed to really miss his master. He would sit by the door, wagging his tail, and sometimes he would let out a long depressed sigh. He didn't eat as much and was not interested in his toys. Florence took him out for a few minutes every day, but she did not have the time to run around with him for hours like John used to. It occurred to her the two probably slept together most nights, John on the tiny sofa in the snug, Spencer curled up at his feet. They had had a whole independent dynamic going on, which she knew nothing about. She thought about shipping the dog to John, but she couldn't do that to Tim. Spencer was a beam of light in Tim's life, his only friend. His furry brother, in a way. That made Florence love the dog more, as an extension of her love for her son.

The other thing was, now she lived alone, she was in love with the house again. Over the two days since John had left, she had barely slept trying to fashion it into the sort of place a single woman and a child might call home. She'd had a big sort-out: weeded out John's things, old keepsakes of their life together she wanted to forget, cool city-girl clothes she could not even stand looking at. There was a green silk dress she'd almost thrown out a few months prior that had made it back into her closet. She used to wear it to go wine-tasting with John when they'd first moved in together. It slipped off her thin shoulders, becoming more and more revealing throughout the night. It was John's favourite. She'd stuffed it in a rubbish bag as hard as she could and resolved to never think of it again.

After the clear-out, she'd felt much happier. She'd turned the snug into a mini playroom, which freed up the rest of the house from stray toys. She'd thrown out the toddler bed, where Tim had only slept once since he preferred sharing the bed with her and her growing belly. Now, sitting in the hallway with that last framed memento of her married life in her hands, Florence mostly felt relieved. It was her home again, her nest where she felt cosy and safe. Where Tim could feel safe, and grow up surrounded by love.

The irony was, now that the house was actually pleasant to live in she probably would not be able to stay in it. Based on the internet research that she had done, she knew that she had very little chance of keeping the house unless John was willing to go above and beyond. She wasn't even sure she wanted his charity. In fact, she was pretty sure that she did not. One way or the other, her life would have to change. She felt her baby girl kicking, right below her ribs.

"Yes, baby," she said out loud. "Life will have to change."

11

CLAIRE

They sat in silence, in the darkness, drinking hot cocoa. The estate agent had called right before dinner. There was a problem. The buyers had pulled out. Claire had actually let out a short burst of laughter. Of course they had. All of their possessions were packed, neat stacks of cardboard boxes lining the hallways. They had rid themselves of a literal truckload of stuff. All the children had come back to salvage what they wished to retain from their childhood rooms. They had all intended to keep a box at most, but had made it back home with full cars. Elijah had taken a few days off work and had helped them take dozens of packed plastic bags and cardboard boxes to charity shops, filling up his eco-friendly SUV and spreading out his trips to as many different charity shops as possible.

Most of the furniture was gone, and they were only moving with a couple dozen boxes. They were both currently living out of suitcases, ready for the move. They were eating takeaway pizzas and cold salads a lot, as they had already packed all their cookware and crockery. It was not comfortable, and Claire had realised they were getting too old for discomfort. They were due to move in three days. And yet, there they were. They'd had dinner in silence, and then Claire had unpacked their saucepans and mugs to make them hot chocolate. She couldn't live with the thought of having to re-pack them. They sat in the kitchen, with all the lights off, and drank their cocoa and took turns petting Marmalade. If they'd had any cigarettes in the house, Claire would have smoked one but Michael had thrown them all out as they were clearing the house and she had not yet gotten round to replenishing her secret stash.

Their first thought had been for Aaron. He needed the money in his account by the following week, or the whole project would fall through. No house, no refuge. The vulnerable small children would remain in whatever precarious situation they currently were. They thought about not telling him for a couple of days, try to see if they could figure out a solution. But they quickly agreed that would not work. Aaron wasn't a child who would be disappointed, he was a grown man who had to decide what to do with his future. People's livelihoods were at stake.

Claire had called him while holding Michael's hand; it had been a hard phone call, one of the hardest she had ever had to make. Aaron had cried. Michael had cried. She'd swallowed the tears that were burning a hole in her throat, because she knew she had to be strong for them. Almost immediately, she'd switched to her old reactive mode. They would try to fix this. There had to be a way to fix this. She'd shipped Aaron off with a list of things to do: get in touch with the government. Ask for an extension. Reach out to the people he'd already hired, see if they could start later. Aaron relished having things to do, it gave him something to focus on and calmed him down. Claire knew her son. When Michael was shot, Aaron was only seven. In the long months after Michael had come back from the hospital, Claire had kept Aaron sane with an endless list of made-up tasks.

While Jacob and Elijah spent hours sat on their father's bed, reading him books and newspapers, Aaron needed to work. Claire asked him to dig holes in the garden, then had him fill them back up. She had him fold hundreds of paper squares into quarters, then unfold them. She even had him do laundry, a task most seven-year-old boys would not enjoy but to which Aaron took like a fish to water. Every day, as his father groaned through his gruelling physical therapy regime, he would sit on the floor and fold clothes. Neatly, steadily, his eyes wet with tears and his hands shaking.

After giving Aaron tasks, Claire had turned her attention to the matter of the house. She'd called the estate agent and explained the situation. They had to find another buyer as soon as possible. The agent had seemed genuinely sorry for them, but had also been honest. It would be difficult, she'd said. With the market being where it was, there were not many people wanting to take on a house like theirs. Claire knew what she'd meant was a project, a lovely home in sore need of renovation. Plus, their house was expensive. Not many people were looking for a five-bedroom home, and even fewer people could afford it. The agent seemed willing to try, but Claire knew that there wasn't much hope. They had been such idiots, Michael had said. Banking their son's dreams on a sale that could fall through at any moment. That was Michael, blaming himself for situations entirely out of his control.

When Claire's first book had come out, her publisher had thrown her a small dinner party at a fancy restaurant in central London. They had left the children home with a sitter, one of their friends, and had gone up on the train. They'd had a wonderful time: Claire was ecstatic and Michael was ecstatic for her. By the time they'd come home, they had both been rather tipsy. They had quickly sobered at the sight of cold blue ambulance lights in front of their house. They had run in, their hearts full of panic and their minds full of worst-case scenarios.

It was not a big deal: Jacob and Aaron had been wrestling and Aaron had slipped and broken his arm. The babysitter had panicked and called an ambulance. She was in floods of tears; she'd been giving Gideon his bath upstairs and had not thought to separate the other boys.

Jacob was equally heartbroken, sobbing on the stairs like the world was ending. He had rushed towards Claire and had burrowed his face in the soft silk of her evening dress, smearing snot all over it. On their way to the hospital, Michael had been furious with himself. They shouldn't have gone to London. They should have taken the boys with them, or at least the eldest two. He could have stayed behind to watch the boys. It wasn't just Aaron who was hurt; he was devastated Claire's big day had been ruined. She had needed a fresh start, a new career. This was the beginning of it, and it had now been tarnished. And, at least the way he saw it, it had all been his fault.

So Claire had spent the rest of the evening trying to make Michael feel better about himself. She had reasoned with him: Aaron was a grown man, a doctor, he knew how house sales worked. He had taken that risk, they had merely offered to help. She'd made him a hot cocoa, and they were now sitting in the darkness. Marmalade's soft purr was the only sound throughout the house.

"Honestly, Claire, do you think we will get a new buyer?" Michael's slurring was worse now he had been crying.

"We will, my love. I promise. I'll not let this fail." She felt a strong surge of determination in her chest. She would not allow herself to be beaten down.

"We can have an open house," she continued. "Invite everyone we know. We can ask for help from the boys, they must know loads of people looking to move to the country."

"That's a good idea." Michael stroked her hair.

"The estate agent said the sellers of our flat will probably wait a couple of weeks before looking for another buyer," Claire carried on, mostly talking to herself. "This can still all work."

"Worst-case scenario," said Michael. "We can just rent somewhere for a bit and find a new place to go."

"Are you sad at the idea of missing out on the flat?"

"Not really, no. I guess maybe that's something I should think about." He frowned. "Are you?"

"Do you know – I was just thinking about that." Claire scratched a spot behind Marmalade's ear. "I was not half sad about it. I mean, I don't really care. And I've always cared about our house before."

"Maybe this is a different stage of life. It will be more about what we do than where we do it." Michael did not sound too sure.

"Yeah, maybe."

They sat in silence, until Marmalade had enough and jumped off Claire's lap. He scuttled towards his litter box, his full tail gently swaying like a flag in the wind.

"Claire," said Michael, slowly, "if it wasn't for Aaron, would you be upset about the buyers pulling out?"

She thought about it. She cocked her head to the side and took one sip of cocoa. It was almost cold and reminded her of chocolate milk. Her boys had loved chocolate milk when they were small. In the summer, she would make a great big batch and keep it in the fridge in a glass jug. It would always be gone by morning, and her children would sport a cheeky chocolate moustache as they denied all involvement in the milk's disappearance.

"No," she said softly. Michael didn't respond, but he reached out and held her hand. He squeezed it in his, her long and delicate fingers disappearing in his large palm. He got up and kissed her on the top of her forehead.

"Let's go to bed, dear," he whispered. "Tomorrow will be better."

☙

The next day started off well. The estate agent called: they were putting the house straight back on the market.

"I'll put a picture in the shop window, Claire," she said. She was a sweet girl, and Claire had learned she was even a fan of her books. She was eternally baffled at the existence of people who not only read, but appreciated her books and wanted to talk to her about them. The first time her agent had asked her to do a reading in a bookshop, Claire had been more than prepared to sit in an empty room. Instead, it had been quickly filled by people who called themselves her fans. Mostly women, and younger men. They had listened to her read, and one or two of them had even cried. They'd queued up neatly, waiting for her to sign their copies of her book. As she had looked at their faces, Claire had suddenly realised that she was, to some extent, famous. Although it had been over thirty-five years since that first signing, she still struggled with the idea.

She had never reached the level of fame where people recognised you on the street or at the supermarket, but whenever she ran into somebody who enjoyed her books, Claire was perennially surprised. The estate agent, to make matters worse, seemed to be a genuine fan. She had given them what Claire suspected was preferential treatment. And now she was doing it again, giving them a prime spot in the office window and offering to call around her clients, trying to entice as many people as possible to come see the house.

Around lunchtime, Claire unpacked a few of their kitchen things and made lunch. She had recently been on an Italian cookery course, and she was feeling inspired. She was making gnocchi with a creamy mushroom sauce, and a crisp salad. They deserved a good lunch. Plus, Aaron was coming down and she wanted to treat him. She was glad she had cooked something special when he came through the door, looking almost cartoonishly deflated. He didn't even take his shoes off, and plodded towards the kitchen. He sat down at the table, his eyes red from the lack of sleep and possibly tears, and accepted the glass of water his mother was offering him.

"We have three weeks, Mum," he said, in a hoarse voice.

"Who did you speak to?" Michael asked, as he came in from the garden. He had cut down a great big cluster of pink hellebores and Claire could not help but smile. He knew they would cheer her up.

"I spoke with the grants officer in charge of our project," Aaron replied, as Claire put the flowers in a cut-crystal vase she fished out from one of the open cardboard boxes.

"What's his name?" Michael asked. He knew people, even though more and more of the people he knew were retired, or dead.

"Peter Bottani," Aaron replied curtly. He was annoyed, Claire thought. She probably would be too.

"We have three weeks," Aaron continued. "After which they need to see either another offer on your house, or the money. If not, well, it's over." He pounded a fist on the kitchen table, which rattled. Michael raised his eyebrows. Claire just stood there, clutching her vase. She was not prepared for an outburst.

Aaron looked at both of them and shook his head, his expression blank. "I'm sorry," he said in a small voice.

"That's all right, darling," Claire said with excess cheerfulness as she sat down. "We are doing everything we can. Just in case, is there anywhere else you could get the money?"

He shook his head. He looked about ten years older than the last time she'd seen him. "Nowhere, Mum. It's far too much money. We have already been through everyone we know who might help, and there's nothing anyone can do."

Michael smiled as he put his hands on her shoulder. "Well, son," he said with pride. "Your mum is doing things about it. She's all over it. Have faith."

They both smiled. Michael and Aaron had such blind faith in her, in her ability to magic things out of thin air. Claire used to relish it, her family name as a problem-solver, a magician of impossible tasks, but this was a bit too much pressure. She sought to distract them.

"I thought we could do an open house this weekend," she said. "Invite everyone. The estate agent was quite positive, she said she would send us some good prospects. I think the key problem is, nobody your age would want to live in this house without doing some serious work to it." She made a sweeping gesture, encompassing the dated kitchen, the brightly coloured walls and the tiny hallway. "So we need to make it look more modern."

"We could paint the kitchen white," Michael suggested. He'd listened to every couple coming through their home and knew that a kitchen that wasn't white, dark blue or green appeared to be unacceptable.

"Calm down, Dad." Aaron looked up. He seemed irritated. "There's no need to go painting things. It won't dry in time and the colour of the cabinets is the least of your problems."

Claire sensed a clash coming. The mother of four boys and the wife of one, she knew how to redirect. "Lunch anyone?"

They ate at the kitchen table, helping themselves to gnocchi from the large round casserole dish she placed in the middle. She had a big bowl of salad, and a basket with small bread rolls studded in sunflower seeds. Carbs made everyone calmer.

❧

After lunch, she magicked some Cornettos from the freezer.

"Hey, Mum. Do you remember the Italian ice cream story?" Aaron asked, a white moustache forming over his upper lip.

She smiled. On their way back from Egypt, they had once been forced to go home by land. No plane seats available. They had taken a ship to Italy, and then sat for long, exhausting hours on the clanking trains that run from the sole of the boot all the way up to the Alps. The children had eaten nothing but gelato, which had eventually made them sick. Once they'd got home, their grandmother who had come to greet them at the station had offered to take them for ice cream when she met them from the train. She had been baffled by their emphatic distaste for that idea. It was still an old family joke they all shared every time gelato was mentioned. Elijah and Tom had even had a gelato stand at their wedding, and the gelato story had been told during Michael's speech. Michael, Claire and Aaron all smiled silently, eating away at their cones.

Claire's mobile rang.

It was the estate agent. They had a viewing, now. They would be over in an hour. There was no time to run around, make the place look nice.

"We'll just go for curb appeal," Aaron decreed. "Be honest. If they want this place, it's to renovate it. Totally gut it and redo it. They won't care it's a little messy."

Claire felt wounded that her son couldn't even conceive of someone loving their house as it was. Looking at Michael, she could tell he was too. They had done everything to make this a magical family home for Aaron, and he seemed to not care much for it other than a form of income.

Yet, he was right. The couple who came were in their late thirties and seemed to be much happier than the first couple who had put in an offer. They held hands and talked about how they would change the house to make it their own. It was clear from the sparkle in the wife's eyes that she was in love with the place.

"I know I shouldn't say this," she whispered conspiratorially, "but this really does already feel like home."

Her husband told her off, gently, but Claire could tell he was smiling at the corners of his mouth. "Could we keep chickens?" he asked.

"Of course! We used to have a chicken coop, right in that corner by the pear tree."

"How wonderful for the kids!" The wife squealed.

Claire and Michael looked at each other. It was done. They had them in the bag. They offered tea, and the estate agent and viewers spent a few more minutes standing in the middle of the garden, sipping from their mismatched cups and pointing at the back of the house. Claire, after a lifetime of living with Michael, could read lips very well.

"Oh honey, I love this," said the woman.

"Me too," replied the man. "I just don't want to be too impulsive. It would need work."

"We can afford it!" she replied. Her cheeks were flushed in the autumnal air. "And we can do it bit by bit. It may take a few years, but it will be so worth it!"

He laughed and put his arm around her shoulder. Claire turned round and smiled to her husband and son.

"I don't want to be too cocky," she said with a twinkle in her eye. "But I think it's done."

They put in an offer a week later. It was incredibly low, well below asking price, but it was a start.

"They probably just want to play hardball," said Elijah. He had come down with his son, Lukas, to stay with his parents for a long weekend. Elijah's husband, Tom, was at a stag weekend and Lukas loved to spend time with his grandparents. Claire was pleased, as Elijah had a steady head and generally gave good advice. He and Tom ran a successful GP practice, and he was a volunteer governor at his local primary school.

"Should we play hardball, too?" asked Michael.

"I don't think so, Dad." Elijah exhaled, and sat down. He looked as though he was exercising patience. "Mum, Dad, you know how much I love this house. I love everything about it, because it's my childhood home. And to me, it's an extension of you, and I love you so much."

Claire smiled. Quite a change from how Aaron had tried to say the same thing. She would never cease to marvel at how her children had turned out so different from one another.

"But even though I love it, we love it," continued Elijah. "This house is not what people my age want to buy. I know it sucks, but that's just the way it is."

Michael put his hand on his son's shoulder. He smiled. "Son, we know."

Elijah sighed with relief. "I reckon, call them back and counteroffer something reasonable. Like halfway between what they said and asking price."

Claire obeyed. She found it increasingly soothing to let go, allow her children to take control of things. Jacob had recently accompanied them to one of Michael's doctor's appointments and had asked very good questions. Elijah had mostly emptied their house, culling their possessions ruthlessly just as she wished she could do herself. She was so proud of her sons, of what great help they were. She could relax and let go a little.

In the evening, Claire and Elijah cooked together. It was another of their shared passions. It was more than a hobby, it was a way of showing love. They cooked and baked together, no matter what else was going on in the world. It had all started with home-schooling: Elijah struggled with reading and Claire had asked him to read recipes out loud as she cooked. She would purposefully forget details so he had to go back quickly and figure out how many onions and how much flour was needed. From there, it was their special bonding time. In a family of six, one-on-one time was precious.

Elijah had come out to her when he was seventeen in that very kitchen, as they were baking a cake. Claire had been very surprised: he'd always had girlfriends wherever they went, leaving a trail of broken hearts in the homes of aid workers and diplomats across the Third World. Claire had never cared about whether her son was gay or straight, but she had always been afraid he would not be able to find the same kind of bond she had found with Michael, and that he would not be able to experience being a father.

As they stood in the kitchen, making polenta with a rich beef stew, she watched Elijah teach his son how to peel shallots. She smiled. She had been so wrong. Elijah had found true happiness with Tom, and since having Lukas he had shown what a wonderful caring father he was. She should never have worried about him. He was such a kind resourceful man. He had been relentless with the adoption system, fighting to get on the right lists, demanding to be heard and to be seen. Lukas had come to them a baby of six months, terrified of strangers and getting over a heartbreaking drug addiction he had developed in his birth mother's womb. Six months later, he was a happy and confident one-year-old safe in the firm love of his parents. Now, as a four-year-old, he was the light of their lives. He was a giggly, mischievous boy who loved to play with his truck toys and who astounded them all with an expansive vocabulary.

They had just finished peeling the pink shallots for the stew when the phone rang. It was the landline. Elijah picked it up and frowned. He gestured to get her to come over.

"It's for you, Mum. It's the estate agent. Your mobile is off." Of course it was. She always forgot to charge it, it must have died in her purse. Or maybe in the hallway. Finding the damn thing now would be impossible, as she couldn't ring it.

"Hello?" she said into the receiver.

"Hello, Claire. This is Tina with Bevindale's Property." Her voice was hesitant. "I'm afraid I have some not-so-great news."

"Oh?"

"Unfortunately the buyers have rescinded their offer." It was the second time she had to hear that in two weeks. That was just too much. Claire sat down.

"Oh, right," she said, her mind racing. "I mean, we would be open to further negotiating the price," she continued with a feeble voice.

"Oh Claire, I am so sorry," said the agent. "The offer they put in was at the very top of their budget. I don't think they have any wiggle room at all. Look," she lowered her voice, "if I thought they could budge, I would tell you. But I really don't think they can, all the other properties we have shown them are, well, far below yours in terms of price point."

Claire did not know what to say.

"I'm so sorry, Claire," the agent continued. "I know how much this meant to you and your family. But look, this isn't over, we'll keep trying!" She was striving to sound cheerful. That made it worse.

"Right, well thank you, Tina," Claire said slowly. She felt like she was in a terrible dream and would wake up any minute in her new apartment in a glass building in London.

"Thank you, Claire. And don't worry, we'll figure something out. Have a good night."

"You too, Tina." Claire hung up the phone. A heavy silence had fallen on the kitchen. Michael was stood in the doorway, trying to read the emotions on her face.

Claire buried her face in her hands. "It's over," she said.

"Elijah, please call Aaron and ask him and Penelope to come down."

Michael put his arm around Claire's shoulder and kissed her. She cleaned her face on her apron, which smelled of vanilla extract and mushrooms. She drew in a deep breath, feeling as though she had failed her son. Now she had to tell him to his face.

12

ALEX

The sale had fallen through. Last minute. Well, almost. Their buyers had lost their buyer, and the estate agent had pleaded with them to allow a little time. Cash buyers don't come every day, he'd said. He was an unpleasant man, with a gammony red face and too-wide ties in colours that should be kept for brothel neon signs. Nevertheless, Sarah agreed with him. She had taken a shine to their buyer, who was apparently somewhat of a famous writer. They had googled her name while they were dealing with all the paperwork, and it turns out she had written a lot of books. Good books, apparently, as Sarah had even found the time to read one on her Kindle during her evenings and weekends. Up until a few weeks earlier, those would be peak job-hunting hours, but no more. She had simply stopped looking. Alex knew why. It was because of their fight.

He had used her phone to look something up, and discovered she had been scouting a small family PR firm in New Jersey. Not, as she said she was doing, big names in the city, but a small firm hours away from the hustle and bustle of Tribeca. Somewhere where men didn't have to wear a suit. A family-friendly workplace, as the "About us" section of the website promised. He had confronted her, trying not to be too direct. He had not accused her of wanting to settle down and have children, just of throwing away her career.

She came right back at him, pointing out that there were no jobs like she wanted in New York at that moment. The argument had circled right back to where he really should have suggested getting married to buy her more time to find a job. He had said nothing. She had said nothing. They had gone to bed, and they had woken up the next morning ready to reconcile. They had both apologised, and had gone for a sterile walk in Greenwich Park.

After the argument, their relationship seemed to shrink. They talked less, because they knew another argument was looming right around the corner. They still discussed their work and had meals together. They went out for brunch with their friends. They went to the movies at the BFI, and to music gigs all over London. They tried new restaurants after reading reviews online. They did all the things they normally did. But it was not the same. Alex loved her so much, but was so scared to ask her whether or not she was about to leave him for someone who would give her a baby. He felt as though she was constantly staring at him with her dark piercing eyes. Sometimes he would turn around and find her looking at him intently, furiously and quietly like a mad painting.

So they would give the buyers about a month before they looked for someone else. It didn't really matter, Sarah said, as she was still looking for a job. Whether she did so from their flat or from her sister's house, it was irrelevant. Alex was somehow relieved that the burden of packing and moving had been lifted from his shoulders. He still, more and more feebly, hoped that he would move and a few weeks later Sarah would surprise him at his New York apartment, throwing her arms around his neck as she told him she had found a job. Not only that, but that she had been a fool to ever doubt their life, and that she did not, after all, want three children and a dog. With every day that went by, Alex knew that would never happen. He could see it in her face, studying him with calm contempt. *She must think I am a real piece of shit. She probably thinks I have taken advantage of her, and I am refusing to marry her and get her pregnant like I am supposed to.* He was starting to get angry too.

At any rate, the plan seemed to be going ahead. Alex would move to New York on his original date, Sarah would sort out things in London, get a job and follow as soon as possible. It was becoming ridiculous they weren't getting married. They had lived together for fourteen years, and now they were about to live apart for an unspecified period of time. Could be years. Their friends seemed surprised, many confused. They inquired, politely, and after a few drinks more and more cheekily. Kelly, his best friend at the firm, got very drunk one night and told him square to his face he was ruining his life. She had just come out of a bad long-distance relationship and was jaded about it all from the start. She adored Sarah, and was angry at him for not doing the sane thing.

"Rent the flat out, get married and hop over the pond, man," she said, slamming her chubby hand on the back of his perfectly manicured head. "Long distance never works. It never, ever works," she repeated, with a slither of bitterness. He believed her, but felt powerless to do otherwise. To ask Sarah to marry him now, he felt, was to sign up for a life he did not want. A large house in New Jersey, white picket fence, Labrador puppy and two children. He would commute every day into the city and hate himself so hard he might actually jump off from a tall building. And there was always that tiny hope that Sarah would appear at his door, happy and elated, eager to resume their old lives.

He was thinking about Kelly's words in the cab he was

sharing with Sarah as it slowly made its way to the airport. Sarah had insisted on coming with him to say goodbye, which is sweet in films but an absolute nightmare in real life. The car sat in traffic somewhere near Hounslow, inching forward with a gentle back-and-forth motion that made Alex sick. Sarah was leaning over, furiously typing away on her Blackberry. She was technically off work, but work never stopped.

Alex looked up from his own email-filled phone at her beautiful, thin, symmetrical face. The thick brown fringe that covered her forehead made her eyes look huge, like a doe's. He would miss her, he thought. He already missed her, he realised. The old, happy, ambitious, funny Sarah who had gone missing slowly, day by day, over the past few months. He thought about saying something. This could all be a terrible misunderstanding. But of course it wouldn't be, and if he said something now they would have a fight and not have enough time to make up, which would be a horrible start to their long-distance relationship.

Instead, they sat in silence, listening to each other's typing and to the driver's screeching LBC until they got to the airport.

"Would you like to go for a coffee?" Alex asked, thinking of the Costa outside of Terminal 5. "I have time."

"I'd better not," she replied, an infinite sadness in her voice. "I need to get back."

They stood in front of each other. She was wearing a teal coloured jumpsuit under her black coat, and a black suede belt that matched her shoes. Her eyes were full of tears, and so were his.

"I love you." *Come with me*, he thought. *I don't care about this anymore. Let's get married and have a baby, if that's what you need.*

"I love you too," she said, her voice breaking. They held each other, their bodies slowly shaking. Alex could feel a solid lump in his throat.

She came apart, looked at him and raised her hand, slowly wiggling her fingers.

"I love you," she said. "Goodbye."

"I'd better go, before I can't anymore." He turned and started walking towards the terminal, dragging his heavy suitcase. *Stop me*, he thought, *run after me and stop me. Kiss me and tell me not to go and I will stay, and we will get married in a small church in Cornwall and buy a three-bed semi-detached in Canada Water and raise two sets of twins.*

She didn't stop him.

He made it until past security before he broke down. He cried for a few minutes in the men's toilets. Then he splashed some cold water on his face, and made his way out onto the terminal. He could go to Wagamama's, Soba noodles for a broken heart.

His phone rang. It was Sarah.

"Listen," she said, before he could say anything. "Listen and don't interrupt, because I don't think I can do it otherwise."

"Okay," he said, knowing what was coming. He sat down on the ground, next to his hand luggage.

"I love you," she said, with a broken voice. "I love you so much it hurts. But I don't think we want the same things in life anymore, and I don't think it's fair on either of us to stay together."

He swallowed hard. He thought he would be devastated, but he felt oddly calm. He felt hot though, boiling under his suit. His face felt like it was on fire. "I know," he said softly.

"I'm so sad," she whimpered, a small voice at the end of the line.

"We should talk more tomorrow. But you're right. This is not fair, and I love you and want you to be happy."

"I'll call you tomorrow to sort things out." Her voice was flat, completely monotone.

"Any time." He leaned his head against the phone. "Sarah?"

"Yes?" There was a glint of hope in her voice that broke his heart.

"I'll miss you, Sarah," he said softly.

"I'll miss you too." She hung up. It was done. He felt a sense of relief. His heart was pounding, but he felt as though the Damocles sword that had been hanging over his head for months was finally gone. He had to break it off with the woman he loved, his partner in life. It was horrible. At least it was done. He got up slowly and limped towards Wagamama's like a wounded toy soldier.

The subsequent week was filled with more phone calls. They were mostly about the admin required to disentangle a fifteen-year relationship. They had a shared expense account they needed to close, and of course there was the matter of selling the flat and splitting the equity. Sarah seemed cold over the phone, detached, as though she was speaking to him through a mirror. He knew what she was like, he knew that was how she protected herself from the pain. The day her grandma had died, she had insisted they stick with their previous commitment of going to a hip-hop brunch in east London, and then pints with friends. She had acted entirely naturally, as though nothing had happened.

When he confronted her in the toilets of the pub, she had broken down. She pretended she didn't feel the pain to numb herself against the great big wave of grief. At least, that was what he hoped. A small part of his brain, one he could not quiet down, kept suggesting an alternative scenario. A scenario in which she was secretly relieved to be rid of him, so she could start looking for someone else. Someone who shared her new life goals. The thought disgusted Alex, and filled him with unexplainable anger.

He tried to throw himself into his work. In many ways, it was the ideal distraction: he spent a lot of time trying to learn the new ways of the New York office, and was taken out for wining and dining most evenings by his new colleagues. Depressingly, he had been right about the move. The work was faster paced, with bigger clients and more exciting stakes. His new boss was hands-off. His new colleagues all appeared to be great fun, and all seemed like potential new friends. And the city was magical. His new friends took him for cocktails in Midtown, and for Ramen all over the city. They went to a speakeasy that still had its original password system at the door, and where everyone drank champagne laced with vodka. This was the life. He started looking online for apartment listings, before realising it was probably time to rent. He went to a few viewings, but the corporate accommodation he was currently in was very comfortable and he did not feel as though he was in a hurry.

This was everything he had hoped for, and more. Only, he had hoped to share all this with Sarah, like he had everything else for the past fifteen years. On the other hand, he realised, moving was the best way to help him heal from the breakdown of his relationship. Every square inch of London was branded with Sarah's face, at least in his mind. On the other hand, they had never been to New York together: the city was a blank slate. He could go where he wanted, dine where he wanted and speak to whomever he wanted without fear of running into her, her friends, her colleagues or just places where they had shared a magical mundane moment. He could feel himself getting lighter, day by day.

Through the whole slow process of breaking up long distance, they only had one fight. This was after a couple of weeks, when she rang him to confirm she had transferred over his half of their shared savings. He had had too much to drink at a work party, and was missing her more than ever. He stupidly pulled out a photo of her to look at while they were talking. It was a somewhat inappropriate picture, taken while she was reading a book on a beach in Croatia. He had focused on her, blurring the background to two broad stripes of white sand and bright blue sea. She was wearing large black sunglasses, a floppy straw hat and a red-and-white gingham bikini, and was engrossed in a book. She always loved those fluffy trashy books you can get in airport bookshops, which used to annoy him and even slightly embarrass him but which now seemed like a small endearing quirk only he was privy to.

He watched her picture as she spoke, monotonously going through reference numbers and exchange rates. He looked at her cheekbones, wrinkled in laughter as she read, he now realised ironically, her terrible book. He missed her so much.

"Listen," he burst in, interrupting her. "I miss you. Let's just forget all of this. Let's do it. Let's have a baby. We can get married, you can come over next week."

"What?" She sounded metallic, almost like a robot.

"Give your notice and leave next week." He was speaking faster, realising the enormity of his mistake as he listened to the words come out of his mouth. "We can get married at the New York Courthouse. Or have a real wedding, whichever one."

"And have a baby?" She was practically whispering.

Was it too late to pull back? Probably. He should pull back now, before he committed to something he would never be able to go ahead with. And yet, he heard himself say, "Yes, Sarah. Have a baby. Start a family."

"Alex?" He could hear her voice quavering. "How dare you."

What? She was meant to be elated!

"How fucking dare you!" she screamed over the phone,

causing his head to heat up. "Where do you actually get off, saying shit like that?"

The argument carried on for a few minutes. More than an argument, it was her shouting at him about how she did not want this, had never wanted this and that if he had ever loved her, ever understood her, ever listened to her, he would know how deeply she did not see herself, or their relationship, that way. Then, after one particularly long bout of shouting, she hung up on him. She texted him a few minutes later. "We should do the rest of the admin by email. It's probably for the best." Alex rolled over, in a drunken stupor, and went to sleep.

The next morning he went for a jog through the city, the cold air hitting his face as he strode through the geometrically arranged streets. He looked at the bare tree branches against the merciless, cold blue sky. He stopped at a street cart to pick up a coffee, and walked back to his apartment.

He could see now what an awful choice he had made the previous night. He did not mean it. He did not want a family, and Sarah knew that. She was letting him go, so he could have his freedom and the life he always wanted. She must have thought he was offering to give her a baby, and a wedding, and all the things he did not want out of pity. More than anything else, Sarah loathed to be pitied. That was why she hid her feelings so deep down, and why she never let anyone know how truly they had wounded her.

She wanted him to want a family with her, he now realised. She wanted him to be excited, to dream about it, to ask her to marry him on a bended knee not because it was tradition, but because he was truly begging her to please, please love him and raise his babies. All he had to offer was love of a different kind, and any attempt at trying to give her what she wanted would be forced, unauthentic and, worst of all, short lived. You cannot live a lie for your whole life, Alex thought as he made his way back into the safety and impersonal cosiness of his corporate apartment. He shook his head in sadness. He had never wanted to hurt Sarah, and yet there he was.

He texted her back: "You're right, let's do email. I am really sorry about last night BTW, I was drunk and not really myself xx."

She texted back almost immediately. She must have been right by her phone, waiting for him to reply. "That's okay. I'll email you next week once I have closed the bank account."

No kisses. No friendliness. Just as well. They were an ocean apart, and worlds apart as well. They only spoke once more, a month or so later. She texted him during what would have been the middle of the night for her. She wanted to talk. They arranged a call for the next day. By that stage, Alex had reached a place where he had moved on enough to know not to hope for a complete change of tune. She was not going to tell him she had got a job in New York and that she wanted to resume their old lives together.

In fact, the more time went on, the more Alex was coming to terms with the fact that from now on, his life would not have Sarah in it. Nevertheless, he was nervous about what would happen next. He shouldn't have. It was a strange call: she asked how he was, told him about her work. Had a brief chat about their common friends, what they were up to, and about their respective families. After about ten minutes they hung up. It was the sort of conversation you have with remote acquaintances you find yourself trapped with on a train; boring, stale and quite stiff. Why had she wanted to do that? Alex knew he would never know, and was starting to accept that.

Right after that phone call, he started slowly and truly

moving on with his life. He left the corporate apartment and rented a small, one bedroom flat right by his work. It was, much like his old one, almost entirely green glass with interesting views over the bowels of the city. He put more effort in his new friendships, and signed up for an exclusive online dating service. He knew he needed someone else to help him get over Sarah. Day by day, he found himself thinking about her less and less.

Over the coming months, his life came together, just the way he had imagined it when he was living in London and was trying to sell Sarah on the idea of moving to America. He was exploring New York, making new friends and even venturing further afield. He went to Florida a lot for work, and spent Thanksgiving weekend at the family home of one of his new friends in Maine. It was magical. He planned a short break for himself and a new friend at the Atlantis Resort in the Bahamas. He never saw her again after they got back to the city, but he enjoyed it immensely and did not think of Sarah once the whole time he was there.

His work was challenging, and he loved it. His new clients appreciated him, his boss liked his work. He pulled many all-nighters, but out of his own volition. He loved to work hard and play hard, and made sure everyone at the office knew it. One of the partners tapped him on the shoulder one day and let him know he knew he had a long and fulfilling career ahead of him. Sarah started being more and more of a memory, a distant shadow he would think of often, but with decreasing frequency. He surprised himself by thriving without her.

13

PAUL
FALLOUT

The sellers were clearly not changing their minds. It had been three weeks, and he'd not heard a single word from them. He'd rung the estate agent twice, and there was no chance of anything happening.

"To be honest, mate," he'd said on the other end of the line, "I really don't think there's anything else we can do here."

It was polite code for please piss off, I have a lot of other customers to attend to. People who might actually buy a house. Paul should have been heartbroken. His dream home, gone. He was a couple of thousands of pounds out of pocket for various fees. He was technically homeless, living in a cottage in Hatfield Peverel that was literally falling apart. While he should have been on the road to getting his life back on track, he was going nowhere fast. On the other hand, he was the happiest he'd been in two years. More than that, he was probably the happiest he'd ever been. Even at the peak of his relationship with Alice, he had never felt this way. He was giddy. He was giggly. He was funnier than he'd ever been, his hair looked better than it'd ever had. He was, quite simply, in love.

He had started working from home on Mondays, an option

he'd never taken advantage of before because he'd hated his tiny flat so much. Now, it was an excuse to cook for Holly. She'd come home, covered in drizzle from her walk from the station, annoyed at the train and tired from work, and he could make her feel better with the wave of a hand. Plus, he loved cooking. Warming lentil stew, with pearl couscous and a side of roasted butternut squash, dripping in honey and tiny thyme leaves. An asparagus and sun-dried tomato lasagne, smothered with cloudy layers of pillowy béchamel sauce and sprinkled with Parmesan cheese. Tonight, a stroganoff: succulent chunks of Portobello mushroom, coated in sauce and served on top of fluffy wild rice. There was salad, thin slithers of cabbage and carrot soaking up an apple cider vinegar dressing, with raisins. He'd made sweet potato fries, coated in cinnamon and brown sugar, and a very spicy Siracha dipping sauce.

Alice had never liked him cooking, because it took forever and it made a mess in the kitchen. Plus, she didn't much care about food. She was a decent cook, but did not think twice about shoving greasy slices of freezer pizza down her throat while she revised for her many exams. Holly loved the fact he cooked for her. She said it made her whole day, and from her face that was definitely true. Plus she couldn't cook, but she would help him by washing or chopping or peeling as instructed. At the weekend, they'd made a stuffed cauliflower cheese together and she even seemed like she wanted to learn. Plus, she ate everything. Alice was the kind of maddening vegetarian who only likes three vegetables: carrots (cut into cubes), peas and lettuce. Everything else was carbs. Holly loved everything he made, with such genuine enthusiasm it was impossible for him not to feel flattered.

It wasn't just her discovering his talents. It went both ways. She was an exceptionally talented watercolourist, something he never would have known if he'd never moved in. She kept her colours in a small tin that had once held some old-school mints, and loved to take her thick pad of watercolour paper around the countryside. While in his mind she was very much a London girl, she actually spent most of her time when she wasn't at work roaming the fields by her house. Her bright hair and her even brighter tights were visible through the mud and rotten leaves miles ahead. That was another thing, her crazy clothes. She owned dozens of thick woollen tights that must have been uncomfortable, in every bright colour under the sun. She kept them in the drawer of her granny's vanity, and every morning Holly picked a new pair. She played little games with herself, like having to stick with the first pair she picked. She wore them under tight shorts and equally colourful dresses, many of which looked vintage. For someone who was supposed to save money, she had a lot of nice clothes. This made her more endearing to him, softer, like her childish side had been exposed.

This was different. Paul felt needed. He felt wanted. He felt listened to. He was afraid to even say it out loud. He'd just called his mum, who was embarrassingly probably his best friend, and had intended to tell her all about it. Well, not *all* about it. But then he realised he didn't know what to say. On the surface, he and Holly had been seeing each other for a few weeks. Hardly "phone your mum" territory. On the other hand, they had been very close friends for almost two years, and knew most of what there was to know about each other. What they didn't already know, they were learning by living together. It was as though their relationship had been sped forward, to that comfortable place where you still really fancy each other, but are no longer trying to make it look as though you have a six-pack. So he and his mum chatted about this and that, and Paul hung up the phone with a sense of excitement. He would call her back in a few weeks. Explain.

In the meantime, something new was on his mind.

"Are you looking at other houses, love?" his mum had asked, and he had not known what to say.

Rationally, the best thing to do was to get on with it. Look at some new places, find another one he liked. He had all that deposit money still sitting in his bank account. On the other hand, Paul didn't really want to. Every time he'd go view a house, he would picture his future life there. In the pink house, he'd imagined a life with a thin blonde wife like the woman who lived there. And like Alice. But now he didn't want to imagine a future without Holly. When he would look at a kitchen, he would think of it as the kitchen where he would cook for her. A reading nook by a fireplace would be filled with Holly, reading books she bought in charity shops and drinking litres of very milky tea. A box room could maybe, potentially, one day, be a nursery for her child. Not that he was going to bring this up to her right now, of course.

There was a thud, and the door opened. The room was suddenly filled with Holly. It wasn't just that she was very tall for a woman, leggy, with brightly coloured tights and even more brightly coloured hair. Holly had a presence, an energy that lit up a room.

"Heya!" she hollered, her Essex accent just barely disguised after a decade of hanging out with public-school kids. He had noticed her accent was stronger at home. It made sense to him, it completed her. It was warm, and friendly.

"Hello!" he hollered back, drawing her in for a kiss.

"It smells amazing," she said, while trying to jam the door back to close it. "This door is a bloody disgrace." It was. You had to rugby-tackle it to open it, and shimmy it across the uneven floor to shut it again.

"I wonder how much it would cost to replace it."

She giggled. "Too much. Plus if we do that, then we'll have to sort out the rest of this God-forsaken place." She'd said we! He could have done a little dance of joy, right there and then.

"Why not?" He'd been thinking about this. He was relatively handy and could help. They could make the place much nicer, if not habitable. He told her.

"Well," she said pensively, while sitting on the bust sofa to take off her Doc Marten boots. "I guess I never really thought about putting some real effort into this place. I'm only here to save money so I can go travelling."

"Sure, sure. I mean… don't you have enough money by now? You've been here for a long time!"

"Ah, almost there," she replied with a cunning smile. "Almost there!"

"You know, travelling for two people is a lot cheaper anyways."

She stopped halfway through taking off her shoes, one foot free, the other foot still in. She looked up at him. She was gobsmacked. "Would you like to come with me?" she asked. There was a quaver of emotion in her voice.

"I thought it could be fun."

"Are you serious?"

"I can't see why not."

She jumped up. Her eyes were full of tears, her voice was slightly broken. "This is crazy," she said. "But I think it's just crazy enough to work."

She hugged him hard, hurting his shoulders with her thin hands. *Going away together is a big step*, Paul thought, *but it's really not that big a deal. Is this like a fear of commitment thing?* He thought he'd lighten the mood.

"So where shall we go first, then? I still have two weeks booked off of work next month from when I was meant to be redecorating. We could go to Spain? Or maybe Greece? Somewhere warm, anyway."

She jumped back. Her eyes were dry. She looked confused, and wounded.

"Paul, what are you talking about?"

"Going away. I know it's not a big trip, but it would be nice to start small and see how we go."

She shook her head. "Paul, I'm not going on holiday, I'm going travelling." Emphasis on the word "travelling". What?

"What do you mean?" He started to see.

"I'm taking a couple of years out, to travel the world."

"What the fuck." It wasn't a question, more of a statement. She was leaving? When? And crucially, what had the last month been about then?

What followed was an argument the likes of which he had never even had with Alice. Come to think, him and Alice had never properly fought, not even once. But there he was, arguing. Raising his voice, even. Holly looked so angry, blood drained from her lips that were almost blue, matching her hair.

Travelling had always been the plan. She'd not had the luxury of a proper gap year, like all of her posh friends. She'd spent her year between college and university working as a Dunelm's floor assistant, and delivering pizzas after hours to save some money. Once she'd got to Oxford, she spent every day that wasn't during term time working, re-stocking shelves at the local Sainsbury's. During term, she worked the maximum allowed twenty hours a week, cleaning offices at night. She would go out with her friends, and while everyone hit the kebab van on the way home she put on her grey overalls and go to work. Getting a job in publishing had been a miracle achieved through hard work, dedication and an iron will. She was doing all right now, but she had never got to go travelling. It was the idea that had got her through all those gruelling years.

Paul was angry, because there was nothing he could say. He couldn't even conceive of anyone going through so much. His parents had expected him to go to university, he'd gone to Warwick having never worked a day in his life. His first job was, embarrassingly, his first job out of university. He'd never taken a year out, because seeing the world wasn't much of an interest of his. Both of his brothers had: George had done the ski season in the Alps, Jim had taken buses and hiked through the Andes from Southern Chile to Venezuela. "Going travelling" had never appealed to Paul; it seemed to him like a distraction from real life. He was in a hurry to get to grown-up hood, and couldn't stand to hang around a minute longer.

What's more, Paul was angry because he felt betrayed. Even though he knew it was far too early, he had pictured things in his head. He was so happy, so light around Holly, he imagined it would last forever. And she'd looked so thrilled to see him every morning, so vulnerable with him, he'd imagined she felt the same way.

"But I do feel the same way!" she yelled.

"If you did, you wouldn't want to leave!"

"Are you out of your mind?" she screamed even louder. Her dream, the goal she had been pushing towards for years. She was meant to give that up, for him? After less than a month?

"And you know what makes me even more mad?" she asked, her voice cracking, her eyes filling with tears. "What makes me mad is that I love you!"

They stood in front of each other, silent. They felt the shockwaves of her words.

Paul felt a red mist come over him. He'd never quite understood what people meant by that, but he could barely see as his face filled with rage. She didn't love him. He loved her, but she didn't love him. He was certain of that. If she did, he told her, she would be thinking the same way he was thinking. They could do up the cottage, and it could be an absolutely magical home. A real home for the two of them, with room for a growing family. Floral wallpaper on the walls, a nursery in the spare room at the back. Instead, she wanted to sell it. Put the money in the bank and run away. He knew she wanted children someday. She had said so herself, on one of their drunken nights in the pub when they were still friends. She had even said she would like to get married, to the right person. So why not him?

She looked so wounded, he was afraid she might actually collapse. She was standing on the dusty floor, one foot still in the untied boot, the other clad in her bright yellow tights. There was a hole in the tights, right above her ankle. Paul had never noticed it before, it must be new.

"Not everyone loves the same way, Paul," she whispered in a monotone sad voice. She stuffed her bare foot back into her other boot. "I'm going for a walk. I think it would be better if by the time I came back you were gone."

She grabbed him in a desperate hug, like she was trying to melt her body into his. They stood, their faces millimetres from each other. He could feel her damp lashes on his cheek. Suddenly, his anger voided, like it had been flushed away. He held her tight. She stood back and wiped his cheek with the rough sleeve of her brown tweed coat. It had been her granny's, she'd told him.

Without a word, she turned round and left, through the door she had never managed to close properly on her way in. He looked around him, slowly coming to grips with what had just happened. The cottage didn't look squalid anymore, it was cosy. The small rooms were warm, and the furniture looked like a set of old friends. On the table, the cold dinner. The congealed Stroganoff, the cabbage salad browning with oxidation. The sweet potatoes had wilted, soggy in their own oil. He wiped his eyes with his sleeve, and he noticed his hand was shaking. He had to get out. Go home.

He had barely made it to Kent, catching the last train out of Charing Cross hauling his hastily packed suitcase. His mother had known better than to ask any questions. She held him in a long hug, while she sent his father to make up the bed in his room. She made Paul a hot chocolate, which he could barely touch. They sat at the kitchen table and talked for over an hour. He crawled back to his childhood room, feeling as though he was regressing into the womb. Over the following week, he felt like he was regressing into an even deeper, larval state. Not even Alice leaving had been that difficult for him. His family struggled to understand. So did he.

14

JOHN

This was, to put it mildly, a fucking disaster. John tried to angle his body differently next to his desk, on the thin strip of carpet in between the window and the wall. The sleeping bag he'd found in the cupboard smelled like tyres, and using a rolled-up jumper as a pillow seemed to not work as well as he'd imagined. He sat up and checked his phone. It was five-past three in the morning. God. Everyone should be asleep. He glanced over, out of the window. He had what many may consider an impressive view. He could see the Gherkin, almost completely clad in darkness. The lights of London had mostly gone out, even though a surprising number of cars were still driving around. Mostly taxis. What was he doing here? By now, he was meant to rest in a super-king size bed in a well-appointed en suite master bedroom in Surrey.

Except, he thought, that was probably always a fiction. He and Florence had not shared a bed for almost a year, what made him think they would start again after they moved? He had come to realise, after the past few weeks, that he had projected a lot onto the move. Like they were moving away from their current, terrible marriage and moving into a lovely new one. The sort of marriage people in that type of house had. Florence had told him, during their final argument, how she'd gone back to look at the house. The demented old man was apparently not demented after all, or maybe he was but he still had enough marbles in him to be very sweet to his wife.

"He planted lilac bushes under her window for her," she'd said. "I can't even imagine a world where you would do something like that for me."

He'd sensed this was about more than lilac bushes, but he did not know how to ask her what she had meant. John had never really known how to talk to women. He had gone to an all-boys school and only really had male friends at university and then at work. The only woman with whom he'd had a non-sexual relationship of any length was his mother. He felt trapped, like they were lovers who woke up to find they could now only speak different languages. He was stuck on Farsi, she could only understand Cantonese. At any rate, he thought as he resigned himself to try lying on his other side, even if they had stayed together he still would not have been sleeping with his wife in their bedroom tonight. She would be in there with Tim. He would be somewhere else. Still, the somewhere else was bound to be more comfortable than the floor in front of a floor-to-ceiling window.

The other option, of course, was Corinne's bed. That had been his first choice, where he'd retreated after he'd left home. She'd seemed happy to see him, and sympathetic to his story. They'd sat up all night, and she'd poured him glasses of red wine as he cried and talked and told her his side of the story. She comforted him. The next day, after work, he'd gone back to her place and they had spent quite a few days going back and forth from work to her house. It was a comfortable routine. They ate Chinese takeaway straight from the boxes and got drunk every night. They didn't have much sex, he was not feeling up to it. He felt so grateful he had somewhere to go, someone to talk to who already knew all the sordid details and did not need him to explain. Someone who would not judge him, he told her. He imagined she would probably want him out of the way sooner or later, so he tried to be a good houseguest. He cleaned up the common spaces, he brought her breakfast in the morning.

And then, it had all gone to shit. His parents had come to visit, to check up on him and have a big summit on the situation as a whole. He had an inkling his mother thought Florence may be open to reconciliation. She sure as hell wasn't. At any rate, the plan was that they would come to Corinne's house to collect him and they would be off to a nice Spanish place his father had been to before. They would sit, eat small dishes of fried potatoes and delicious ham, drink a lot of red wine and talk it all out.

"We'll come back here for a nightcap, if that's okay," he'd asked Corinne.

"Of course," she'd replied, and smiled.

Hopefully she would be in bed by the time they got back, he thought, and his mother would not have to actually meet her in person and be faced with Corinne's exuberant youth. God, she was young. So much younger than him. How old? It had been her birthday a few months prior and while John had happily contributed a rose-gold bracelet and an expensive dinner, he was not actually sure of how old she was. Twenty-three? Twenty-four? Twenty? Who knows.

At any rate, there he was. He'd come back from work, showered hurriedly, stuffed himself in a clean shirt he'd forgotten to iron and was just looking for his wallet and keys when he saw her come out of her room. He felt like someone had hit him in the stomach. She had also changed from her work clothes, into something nicer. She thought she was coming to dinner. She was wearing a cream chiffon blouse with a small floral pattern, with pear buttons and a little dusty-pink velvet bow at the neck. It was unlike any of her other clothes, that were all decidedly sexy and mostly black. It occurred to him she might have borrowed it from one of her housemates. He looked down. She was wearing flats. She never, ever wore flats. All of her shoes had either a six-inch heel or were trainers. She was wearing a good-girl costume, something tasteful she thought his parents would like. She was trying to make a Good Impression. She was Meeting The Parents.

Once again, he could hear the words come out of his mouth and immediately knew he was not handling this correctly. For a lawyer, he was not really in control of how he spoke. He knew what to do. Treat her gently, and kindly. Make it sound like it was his intention to have her meet them, but it was too early. Sadly, his mouth did not catch up to his brain. So instead, he said the first thing that popped into his mind. "What are you doing? And for God's sakes, what on Earth are you wearing?"

As he did, he stepped into the kitchen. He was still looking for his wallet. And there it was, on the kitchen table. A bottle of dessert wine, brand new, and four small glasses. A blue dish with clementines. On the stovetop, arranged on a metal tray and ready to go under the grill, four little crème brûlée pots. They were the posh ones, the ones that came in cardboard boxes from the fridge section at the supermarket. She had removed all packaging, in an attempt to make them look home-made. When he'd said nightcap, he'd meant he would have his parents come up, sit in the kitchen and have a quick bourbon from the bottle he had been steadily working on all week. She thought they were entertaining.

Her eyes were suddenly very red, and full of tears. Right on cue, the doorbell rang; they were here and he was standing there like an idiot, with a crying girl and no wallet. Ah, no, there it was. On the kitchen table. She had put it next to his keys, like she had done ever since he'd moved in. He realised, at that very moment, that that was a small act of caring. For a moment, he felt his heart soften. The doorbell buzzed again. He could not be late for his parents. He grabbed his wallet, awkwardly patted her on the shoulder and left.

Upon his return, he had the good sense to cancel the nightcap. It had been an unpleasant dinner anyways, and he did not want it to last any longer than it already had. His parents were embarrassed at the state of his marriage, and ashamed of him. They wanted him to fix it. He'd tried to explain he also wanted to fix it, but that Florence had made it clear she didn't want to be part of that particular experiment. He'd tried to explain how empty and alone he felt. He knew he had ruined his life, he did not need his mother to condescendingly explain that his daughter would now be born in a broken home. The people who had raised him did not seem to much care about his feelings, which hurt him in a whole new way. He felt like a child again. At any rate, he avoided a full-blown argument and made it back to Corinne's flat. He was so preoccupied by his own pain and in his own anger at his parents, he had momentarily forgotten about her.

And yet there she was, sitting on her bed. She had eaten the four crème brûlée pots, and she had drunk the whole bottle of dessert wine by herself. She smelled like sweet alcohol, and vomit. Her hair was matted on the side of her head, her fringe wet and clumping on her forehead. She had stained that ridiculous blouse. Her eyes were covered in thick running black make-up, melted in her tears. For the second time in one week, John had a big blowout argument. He felt his own ability to emotionally connect shrink with every word. He felt betrayed, let down by yet another woman.

He thought what they had was special. He thought it was pure lust, on top of a deep friendship. He thought she understood him, his desire for a happy family life, his hurt at his wife's blatant disinterest in him. He thought she cared for him like a friend, and wanted him like an insatiable lover. Turns out, she was on a different page, in a different chapter of a different book. Different genre altogether. She thought theirs was a love story. She thought he loved her. When he told her he could not wait to see her, he had meant he could not wait to take her clothes off. She thought he'd meant it. In fact, she thought he'd meant all the passionate things he'd said in the heat of the moment, about how she was his match, the missing piece of his puzzle, the only person who could make him happy just with a smile.

While he was sharing his hurts, late at night, in his texts or talking to her in bed, she thought they were falling in love. Maddeningly, she thought he had finally left his wife for her. She thought he had moved in not as a temporary place to stay while he found his feet, but as the next step in their relationship. Apparently, she'd spoken with her housemates about him moving in permanently and contributing to the rent. In all objectivity, she probably had more of a right to feel betrayed than he did.

And yet, he was furious. In a way, this hurt more than his separation from Florence. Corinne had made him feel as though he was not alone. He'd thought he had found a connection, someone who understood him. That had given him faith, that while he was a terrible husband and probably an average father, there was hope for him to be happy again, someday. In fact, he hadn't found a connection. She had misunderstood him as badly as Florence had. He felt crushed. For the second time in two weeks, he shoved his stuff in his duffel bag and left in a hurry. He ran into one of Corinne's housemates on the landing, and she gave him a look that could have frozen him to death. *From her perspective*, he thought, *I am a real piece of shit*. From most people's perspective, to be frank.

He made it to the office, which was only a short walk away. He found his desk, and lay underneath it. He did not sleep a wink all night.

The following day, he had the afternoon off to go talk with his lawyer, make a plan to do with separation, child support, that kind of thing. He could not bear the thought. It seemed like an impossible weight to lift. As he sat at his desk, staring blindly into space, he realised he physically could not go through with it all. The intolerable burden of organising his new life. He felt his hand reach for the first drawer in his desk, which he kept locked. Inside, hidden under a stack of papers, was a small orange bottle. It was from the US, he had brought it back from one of his most recent business trips. It was easy to get prescription pills over there, if you knew who to ask. In it were about eighty pills of Adderall. ADHD medication, something he did not need and could never get prescribed on the NHS but that helped him focus and pulled him through when he could not muster the strength to get on with his life.

He had started taking pills to concentrate in sixth form. He was expected to get straight As, because he went to an unbelievably expensive school where anything but perfection was considered a failure. His parents had sent him there to guarantee his academic success, which meant he really had to do well. The problem was, he did not care very much, and this made it difficult for him to concentrate.

After school was university. He had started partying pretty hard after his first year, and needed help to catch up on his work. He would go out all night, drinking and dancing and making out with girls he barely knew. He would hit the library in the morning, still stinking of booze, and take a couple of pills to help him get straight into the books. He would take a quick nap in the afternoon and do it all over again. He had tried cocaine a few times, but that made him feel dirty. Cocaine was a drug, and drugs were for addicts and people who couldn't get a grip. Adderall was a medication. Sure, it had not been prescribed to him specifically, but it was a legitimate thing legitimate people took for legitimate purposes.

Once he'd started work he had eased back on the pills for a while. Once Tim was born, however, there was nothing he could do to stop himself. Life at a law firm was tough enough, without the added pressure of living a double life. He had to get everything done in time to leave, spend time with Corinne and then make it home before Florence went to bed. He needed the help. And the help came, every time, in the form of those little white pills. Could be allergy medication from the looks of it.

Over the next few days and weeks, faced with an impending divorce, a broken affair and homelessness, John started taking the pills more and more often. He slept in the office for a week, and then found a sub-let of a bedsit a few minutes away from the office. He had no money to spare. After he had gone through his accounts with the lawyer he had realised he would not be able to afford a proper home for many years to come. Florence would have to move out from that stupid little house too, a fact that gave him the perverse pleasure of knowing that while he was uncomfortable and unhappy, she would soon be as well. What's more, work kept piling up on his desk. The longer he spent at the firm the more he realised he hated his job. The next step was always supposed to be when the good times came, but they never did. First, get a job. Then, go on secondment. Then, make partner. And yet, the next step always sucked almost as badly as the one before. Except now he had more money, but the money was rendered useless by his incredibly expensive separation, soon to be an incredibly expensive divorce.

To make matters even worse, Corinne refused to quit her job. So he had to see her every day, looking more beautiful than ever as she stared at him with cold distant eyes. He had hurt her more than he would ever know, he realised, and now she was making him pay for it. He thought of attempting reconciliation, but he could not cope with the idea of how much effort it was going to be. So he just retreated into himself, a shallow existence of work, Netflix and drinking.

In fact, he was drinking more every day. He would go for pints every night, always with someone new. Mostly he managed to find some of his actual friends who wanted to come to the pub, but when he couldn't he would settle for anyone. People he hardly knew from work. People from different offices, but in the same building. Neighbours. After the pints, while the others retreated to the normality of their full lives, he would grab a takeaway and a bottle of wine and finish both in the depressing privacy of his bedsit. Then, he would crack out the vodka. Whenever he could, he would forgo this ordeal in favour of a real night out, with dancing and bartenders and other people. He even tried to hook up with strangers, with almost no success.

He was gaining weight rapidly. He had always been tall and well-built, but all the muscle had been replaced by fat. A quickly expanding beer-belly was beckoning. He even had to buy new shirts, as the old ones strained to contain him. He hated looking the way he looked. He had always been into exercise, and loved to take long runs with Spencer. God, he missed that dog. He missed his wife and child too, but the dog had been his one real companion for over a year. He had thought of taking Spencer with him.

Nobody would miss him: Tim was barely aware of him and Florence certainly wouldn't. She hated that dog. She hated the fact the dog liked him better, and she hated how they had bonded. She hadn't even wanted a dog in the first place, although she had demanded he get a stray from the rescue centre instead of a Labrador. Typical Florence; she had demands about things she didn't even care about. His childhood dog had been a Labrador, and that dog had been his best and probably only friend for many years. Not that she knew. Not that he'd told her, upon reflection. Either way, Spencer could not come to the bedsit. Pets are luxuries for people who can afford them, John realised. How heartbreaking.

Either way, without the dog he lost all motivation to exercise. Combined with the daily takeaways and the binge drinking, this explained his horrific shape. Which explained why he couldn't get any women interested in him on nights out. Not that he cared, his libido had melted like snow in the sunshine. Except on this one night. He was leaving work, feeling blank as always. Actually, his mind was mostly preoccupied with work. As well as his physical and mental health, his standards at work were also deteriorating. He was making mistakes, some of them serious. He had just made one. One of the junior associates had realised in time, and had told him. She was bright and was still up in the office sorting it all out for him. Thank God for ambitious young people.

At any rate, as he was coming out he caught a glimpse of Corinne. She was crossing the road, and she was holding hands with a young man. Probably her age. Tall, lean, with flamboyant hair that flowed down to his shoulders. She was laughing, oblivious to John's presence behind her. She was happy. A gust of wind blew up her open coat to reveal she was wearing a tight miniskirt over black tights. Suddenly, he remembered the way she made him feel. He felt miserable, but also like he needed some female companionship.

He lurked around a few bars, but he quickly realised his fantasy of walking in, finding an attractive young woman in a suit and going back to her place after a couple of G&Ts was just that, a fantasy. He was older than most women there. He was fat. He was sweaty. He probably looked awful. He started back on his way home, when he noticed the ads. He must have walked past them hundreds of times, those smutty brightly coloured stickers that encrusted the sides of old phone booths. He'd probably made jokes about them before. Who uses phone booths anymore? People who are looking for a prostitute, that's who.

He could barely recognise himself as he quickly typed in the number on his phone. The voice on the other end was female, soft and surprisingly kind. She was also efficient. By the time John made it back to his bedsit, he knew to expect company within twenty minutes. He could not think about what he was doing, because he felt as though if he stopped to think he would not be able to go through with it. Bizarrely, he tidied up his room. He popped one more Adderall. He needed to concentrate if he was going to go through with this. He poured himself a vodka. Someone knocked on his door.

After she'd left, he caught a glimpse of himself in the mirror. The neon light coming through the gap in the curtains illuminated his face like a ghost's. He looked like a perverse caricature of his father. John turned round in disgust and grabbed onto the vodka bottle. He'd offered some to the girl, but she hadn't wanted any. She'd been foreign, Eastern European probably, and not very attractive. She was very skinny though, and blonde. She had not looked like she was doing this for a good time. To be honest, neither was he. He collapsed on the floor. Why had he taken that Adderall? The pills meant he was struggling to feel the numbing effects of the alcohol. John took another swig of liquor. His phone pinged him. It was past two in the morning, who could it possibly be? He imagined it might be Florence, lonely at night, begging for him to come back. He let out a stridulous laugh at the idea. He checked his phone.

Fuck.

It was the associate he had left back at the office to fix up his mess. One of the senior partners had noticed she was working late and had gone over for a chat. She had been only too happy to talk to him, desperate to etch her face into his memory. Young kids like that were always trying to be noticed, going above and beyond. One thing led to another, he'd found out what she was doing. Not only that, but apparently John had made a series of other very bad mistakes that had come to light. Very expensive mistakes too. So it was up to him to fix it.

"If you can work out exactly what we need to do by tomorrow morning at ten, she had written in her email, we can go talk to the client and resolve this."

Fuck. He pulled up the attachment on his phone. It was a long document, over two hundred pages, and the lines blurred in front of his eyes. He was supposed to go through it and figure out exactly what needed to be changed. He could barely read. He took a few long sips of vodka from the bottle. Wait, what was he doing? That was not going to help him focus. Focus. He needed to focus. He reached over to his pill bottle, and took two more. Wait, that couldn't be right. Could it?

He stood up. Wow. The room started spinning and he folded onto the floor. He could not seem to focus. He was so thirsty too. He took some more sips from the bottle that was next to him. Oh wait, that was vodka. His phone buzzed again, and with enormous difficulty he lifted it to his face. He couldn't read it. In fact, he could barely make out the screen through his blurred vision.

"I'll just close my eyes," he whispered to himself. "Close my eyes for a few minutes, and then I'll be able to concentrate." He curled up on the floor and rested his head against his arm.

15

MICHAEL

Aaron and Penelope sat at the kitchen table, looking straight ahead. Michael noticed they had not touched each other since they had come through the door. Penelope was wearing a loose grey hoodie with a large bleach patch on the collar, and light-wash jeans. She looked haggard; they both did. How ironic, they had come home from a war zone looking young and happy, and a few months in this country had been enough to beat them down.

They hadn't come when Elijah called. They had taken their time, only making their way to Surrey the following weekend. They seemed to not be able to even look each other in the face. Michael drew a deep breath. Of all the things in this world, the only one he did not feel prepared to help his children with was marital problems. He had never had any. They had been through hell and back, but had never doubted each other. The rest of his boys seemed to have made similarly solid choices. In fact, it had never occurred to him Aaron would have an issue. Penelope was a lovely woman, and the two of them had been so clearly in love, so oblivious to the rest of the world. Michael and

Claire had always been more concerned with their youngest son, Gideon, and his wife, Melissa.

Gideon and Melissa had started seeing each other on assignment: he was a journalist, she was a photographer. For a few years they had been long-distance: he was travelling the world for work, she spent more and more time in London. They saw each other once every few months. Michael had assumed they would eventually split up. Then, she found out she was pregnant and the rest was history. Claire had been concerned: a child is no solid foundation for a marriage, she thought. And yet, they seemed happy. In fact, they had both never looked happier than they did in their quiet suburban lives. Michael was happy to be wrong. On the other hand, the tension between Aaron and Penelope was palpable.

"Darling." Claire reached out to clasp Aaron's hands across the table. He quickly moved away.

Penelope turned towards him. "You need to tell them." Her voice was cutting, like glass.

Aaron took a deep breath with his eyes closed. He looked like he was about to explode. "Mum, Dad, Penelope and I are separating."

"We are not separating," Penelope came right back at him, rolling her eyes with an exasperated flourish. "We are getting a divorce."

"That's the same thing."

"No it's not. If you tell them we are separating, they'll think we want to give it another go."

"How would you know what my parents would think?"

"Oh for fuck's sake." Penelope got up.

Michael realised she must have lost at least a stone. Her face was gaunt, her arms almost skeletal as they peaked through the hoodie sleeves.

Claire continued, with her calm and nurturing voice. "Darling, what's going on?"

"Oh for fuck's sake," Penelope repeated. With a few quick steps, she reached the kitchen door and ran out of it. She tried to slam the door, but the springs were old and all she achieved was the soft sound of plastic hitting against the wall.

Claire stared at her son in disbelief.

That was very out of character, Michael thought. *Not in this family, that's not what we do.* He quickly realised Penelope was not technically a part of his family in that way, she had not been taught the same ground rules he and Claire had laid for their children.

Aaron shook his head and buried his face in his hands. He wasn't crying, he just sat there, silent. Claire got up and sat next to him, wrapping her arm around his shoulder. He looked up.

"I don't need to tell you," he said. "None of this is your fault. Things were already pretty bad in Yemen." Claire rubbed a circular pattern across his shoulder blades, like she used to do when he was a baby.

"Coming home was a last-ditch attempt to make a go of things. The refuge project was an attempt at sharing something again. And for a while it worked, it made us feel like we were working together. But now that's over, we don't..." he waved his arm around. Claire nodded, knowingly. Did she know what he was talking about? Michael also nodded, trying to look sympathetic. He felt his son's pain, but was having a hard time imagining what that was like. He could never imagine not feeling connected to Claire, not feeling like they were part of the same team.

He was so lucky to have her. He put a hand on her shoulder to feel her reassuring warmth, her scent and her presence. Without even looking, she flicked his hand away. Fair enough. Their heartbroken son probably did not need to look at his parents being affectionate. Michael felt very much in the way.

He awkwardly lumbered towards the door. "I'll go check on Penelope." He had no interest in doing so, but he felt this would get him out of having to sit in the kitchen, powerless as his son's eyes filled with tears. Neither Aaron nor Claire looked like they noticed in the least.

Michael ventured outside. It was a blustery day, but he did not want to go back inside for a jacket. He strode out to the garden. *I'll go check the bird feeders*, he thought. That was a job for him. As he walked towards the back of the garden, he recognised Penelope's faded grey hoodie past the fence. She had made it onto the public footpath and was sitting in a clearing in the wood, on the ground, sobbing. He did not want to, but knew he had to go over. If anything, Claire might see him from the kitchen window.

He closed the gate behind him, and walked over. He felt even more useless than in the kitchen, lumbering over his sobbing daughter-in-law and shivering in the winter air. He put his hand on her shoulder, and she looked up. Her face was streaked with tears, her eyes were red raw. She was shaking. It took Michael a few seconds to realise she was looking at him with hatred. He was not used to being hated.

"How fucking dare you?" Penelope screamed.

He took a step back as she shot up.

"How fucking dare you?" she asked again. "Coming here, trying to... to comfort me." She looked disgusted. Michael was distressed, but also very confused. What had he done?

"You, and your wife, and your perfect little lives with your perfect little home. How fucking dare you?" she screamed, folded in half by pain. Michael felt a few drops on his balding head. It was starting to rain. Perfect.

"Penelope?" he asked, trying to sound as clear as he could.

"What happened?" He used to be a professional advocate, a negotiator. And there he was, unable to comfort a woman who by all accounts he should care for.

"Do you want to know what happened? Do you?" she was screaming. The neighbours would hear. Oh dear Lord, what had happened to him that he was now the sort of old fogey who worried about the neighbours?

"Listen," he said quietly. "You can tell me anything. It is my job to listen." It was at moments like these when he wished he could speak properly, so that people could understand him. If he could get through to her, she would listen.

She was somewhere else in her mind, her eyes glazed over. "What happened?" she said with a shaking voice. "Is that I killed my child. Your son and I," she said, her face deformed in a mask of disgust. "We killed my baby. And there is nothing you or I or anyone can ever do about it."

"Penelope, what happened?" Michael asked again.

What *had* happened? She wasn't making any sense. Aaron had never had a child. Penelope was never pregnant. Unless she had been?

She shook her head, walking backwards towards the path. The cold drops had stopped and a gentle breeze was whistling through the bare tree branches.

"I was pregnant, Michael, that's what happened. It was an accident, but we were both so, so happy. And we decided it was a good idea to go on a three-week mission to a refugee camp because, well, because of you!"

"Penelope, I don't know what Aaron told you but we didn't even know you were pregnant... and we would have never, ever told him–" He could feel his words slurring.

"Oh for fuck's sake," she interrupted him. "Of course you didn't tell him to do it. But all his life, all his life he has been trying to live up to your... your legacy." She looked like she had just said a dirty word. "The great Michael and Claire Woodward and their fucking legacy. So he couldn't give up going, because people needed his help. At the expense of his wife and his fucking child. Do you understand? He chose other people's children, over mine. Over his."

As she spoke, yelling over the wind and her own tears, Michael started piecing together what had happened. They were on assignment in Yemen, at a field hospital. Penelope had somehow become pregnant, by mistake. They had both been thrilled. There was a three-week mission to an isolated refugee camp planned, and Aaron had insisted they still go. The pregnancy seemed healthy, and Penelope was strong. She'd agreed. In fact, the more she talked the more she seemed heartbroken about the fact that she had wanted to go. She had wanted to go so much she had lied on their paperwork, denying she was pregnant. Once at the refugee camp, they were dropped off and had to wait three weeks for a pick up.

The first week had been fine. In fact, it had been a success. They were immunising children and seeing people with all sorts of conditions. The days went fast. As the mission lead, Penelope had made sure she gave herself enough time to cool down and rest. Aaron had covered for her where needed. They'd made a good team. Then, they'd all got sick. It was probably typhoid, they'd thought. One night, while they were all up with high fevers, Penelope had started to bleed. The bleeding had not stopped for several days, while she came in and out of consciousness. When she'd finally come round, she was at a military hospital in the UAE. Aaron had fought to get her out, but they'd had to wait for their scheduled pick up three weeks after they had arrived. The baby was gone, and Aaron had authorised an emergency hysterectomy while Penelope was unconscious, to save her life. She would never be able to have children, ever.

They had tried to slot back into their old lives, but to no avail. So they had decided to come back home. Penelope could barely look Aaron in the eye, and vice versa. They had chosen to go, when they could have been much safer staying where they were. Or they could have chosen to go home, immediately, like Gideon had. Instead, they had chosen risk. Michael could not believe that Aaron would ever feel pressured to live up to his and Claire's lives. They had never wanted him to. But maybe, implicitly, they had made him feel as though it was his job to carry on with the family business of saving the world. Gideon was now a journalist covering medical scandals, Elijah was a GP and Jacob had given up medicine for consultancy, which was more lucrative but significantly less noble. Aaron was the only one left doing the type of work his parents had done before him. Working with refugees, wearing bulletproof vests, getting sick and spat at to help others.

Maybe he did feel the pressure. Maybe he had cracked and put Penelope at risk. She had also wanted to go, but Michael imagined she probably did not want to think about that. He opened his arms and she walked straight into them. He closed them and held her for a few long minutes. She had lost so much weight he could feel her bones through her hoodie, her shoulder blades poking him like broken wings. Eventually, she pulled away and turned round, jogging off into the distance up the public footpath. Michael let her go. She needed space. He turned round and went to check the bird feeder.

Once Michael came back inside, Aaron was shouting at his mother. In a different time, Michael would have put him to rights. He had raised his boys with a soft voice, but inside that velvet glove was very much an iron fist. You needed that, with boys. But now, he did not know what to say.

"All I said," Claire was practically whispering, trying to keep calm and not shout, "is that I know, the pain will dull. It will never go away, but you will learn how to live with it."

"Well!" Aaron screamed, his face red, his eyes lit with wildfire. "That was clearly very easy for you, wasn't it, Mum?" He froze. His face fell. He realised what he'd just said, and his mouth opened like that of a dead fish.

Claire also looked frozen. Her face was blank, expressionless. She stood still, and for a few seconds nobody moved. Michael was standing in the doorway, wishing he could run out and forget what he'd heard. Then Claire walked over to her son, looking him dead in the eye. She was moving slowly, deliberately.

She slapped him across the face, in one single blow. It was incredibly loud, and the noise filled the kitchen. They had never slapped the boys, even when they were younger. Aaron didn't move, his eyes were full of tears.

"M--mu--mum," he said, stuttering.

"Please excuse me," she whispered as she turned round and left the room. Michael could hear the creak of the floorboards as she limped upstairs.

Aaron stepped forward. "Dad," he said. "Dad, I'm so sorry, I don't know what came over me. I didn't mean it."

"Get out." Michael made a monstrous effort to make sure his words were coming out clearly.

"Dad, please."

"Get out," Michael repeated. "Your wife is running up the footpath, you might be able to catch up with her. Or don't. In fact, I don't much care where you go as long as you get out of my house."

"Dad, listen." Aaron's tears were streaming down his face.

"Get... out." Michael didn't shout, or raise his voice. His face and body were absolutely still.

"I'm sorry." Aaron grabbed his jacket and headed towards

the front door. "I am really, really sorry. I'll give you some space, text me when you want to talk."

Michael sat at the kitchen table. He could hear the faint sobbing of Claire upstairs. She had locked herself in the master bathroom, he was sure of it. Michael lowered his head on his folded arms on the tabletop, and wept.

16

ESTHER

Esther was born at the Royal Surrey County Hospital on a hot summer's night in 1988. They had just returned from Kenya when they had found out Claire was pregnant, and this time with a girl. They had been overjoyed, finally a baby girl to spice up the lives of their three beautiful boys. Claire had just sold her book, and they had both left the Foreign Office. Michael was going to focus on non-profit work, working with refugees. A new life beckoned.

However, this pregnancy had been full of issues almost from the start. Claire's previous pregnancies had been easy and uncomplicated. She had gained little weight and kept on working and exercising right up to her due date. Jacob had been born in Jerusalem and Aaron was born in England, both in nice hospitals. Elijah, however, was born in rural Kenya, in the kitchen of the large colonial house they had been given to inhabit. All of them had been healthy bouncy baby boys.

This baby was different. She was not growing at the right rate, and Claire kept suddenly bleeding in the middle of the night. She was put on bedrest, given a whole host of extra medical exams. The baby's heart was not working well, they were told. She would probably need surgery as soon as she was born, but she would be all right and go on to lead a happy healthy life. A bump in the road, which Claire had tackled with her usual optimism. She had sat in bed, editing the drafts of her manuscript that her publisher was sending. Michael had looked after the children together with Claire's mum. They'd made it an adventure for them, a little game. A few wild months while Mummy is in bed, followed by a beautiful baby sister to play with.

That bubble had been a ridiculous dream, they had subsequently realised. Claire was just over seven months pregnant when she went into labour. They rushed to the hospital, and Esther was born. But the birth had been too much for her fragile little heart. She lived for six short minutes, before going still and cold in Claire's arms. Those had been the hardest moments in Michael's life. There had been a day, years later in Rwanda, when he knew he was about to die. He had seen the gun, and knew the bullet was coming. That was nothing compared to how he'd felt, wrapping his arms around his wife and looking at their tiny, beautiful daughter turning grey right before them.

Once they had come home, their boys had saved them from despair. They had rallied around their parents, cared for them and hugged them. The boys had given them the will to carry on, to keep being parents and lovers and to work hard to build a better world.

Eighteen months later, they'd had Gideon. They had been on assignment in Egypt when they'd found out, and Michael had asked Claire if she wanted to go home and have the baby there, in the safety of a clean English hospital. She'd shaken her head. She had not needed to say a word, but he knew that she could never go back to where Esther was born. They couldn't save Esther, they didn't get to look after their new baby. Gideon was born, once again, on the kitchen floor, and had filled their hearts with his healthy, lusty cry and his aggressive flailing as they had lifted him up. Beautiful, happy, healthy boy. He had been their last child, and by far the sweetest little boy out of the four of them.

Occasionally, in the midst of the madness that was raising four boys so close in age, Michael looked over at Claire's face and saw a shadow going by. Or she'd raise her eyes and look at him, and they both knew they were both thinking of Esther. The pain had never gone, it had just become part of who they were. They walked past it every day and barely noticed it, like a piece of furniture or a local landmark. People who walk past the Vatican every day to go to work no longer notice it, in spite of how spectacular it looks. Similarly, they just walked past their pain, forgetting what it meant until they thought about it. Michael had been angry, Claire had been broken.

After Michael had been shot, they both saw it as a chance at a new life, a life where they could both be whole. Still, a corner of their heart was always for Esther and always would be. And that's the corner that was throbbing. Where Aaron had stuck his knife and twisted it. Where he'd rubbed his salt. Michael took a deep breath and remembered that quote that used to hang in his office on a little metal sign: "Hurt people, hurt people".

17

SARAH

Once Sarah returned home from breaking up with Alex, she couldn't bring herself to sleep in their old flat. It was hers, it had all of her things in it, and yet she could not make herself put her pyjamas on and get into bed. Instead, she packed a bag and ran off to her sister's house in St Albans. Julia welcomed her with a big hug. They said nothing, just stood in the hallway hugging each other. They were an odd pair: they were never particularly close and enjoyed very different things in life. They even looked different: Sarah in her smart work coat and pointy suede heels, Julia wearing a stained polka-dot nightdress under an oversized grey dressing gown, untied, with the limp belt trailing behind her like a tail. Nevertheless, Sarah felt relief rushing through her body the moment she stepped in the door. She was Getting Away. All of her worries could follow her here, but not as intensely as they did back home. Julia was the oldest, and she was in charge. For this first time in her life, Sarah found it rather comforting.

As they sat in the kitchen drinking cups of mint tea, Sarah reflected on the true power of family. They weren't close, they had very little in common and they had definitely both judged each other's life choices. Julia thought a life without children was incomplete. Sarah felt that Julia's choice to have two children and only work part-time at a non-profit was very much Letting Down The Side. Of course, they had never talked about these things, but they both knew full well how the other one felt. In fact, Sarah was sure that if Julia hadn't been her sister, they would never have been friends. However, none of that mattered, because they were sisters and they loved each other.

Over the coming days and weeks, Sarah came to see her sister and her husband in a different light. They handed over the guest room to her, and a spare set of keys. They did not pry, or ask too many questions, but were always there to help. Every night, when she got home from work, Sarah found a simple but nutritious meal for her under a plate in the kitchen. In the morning, she got first dibs on the bathroom: the children started using their parents' en suite, so she could shower and dress first. In fact, the children were kept very much out of her way. It sounded horrible, but at this particular juncture in time Sarah found it hard to be around them. She loved them, of course, in a cool-auntie sort of way, but they reminded her of her troubles too much. Julia cleared her schedule and found lots of time to hang out with her. She took a day off, and they both went shopping at Brent Cross like a couple of teenagers. It was fun. Sarah bought an ostrich leather handbag, and a silk scarf she was unlikely to ever wear. A couple of evenings they went out for a glass of wine after the children were in bed. St Albans is not much of a nightlife hotspot, but there were a few chain pubs and an All Bar One where they sat and drank bad Pinot Grigio telling funny anecdotes about work. It was nice, in a healing sort of way.

Sarah started feeling better after a couple of weeks at her

sister's place. She had a furious argument with Alex over the phone, when he came out and finally asked her to quit her job to join him and start a family. She had known all along, but to actually hear him say those words hurt more than anything she'd ever felt. This made her so angry: it was such a blatant violation of everything she had ever wanted, everything she had ever shared with him. It was an awful evening; she had called him after a very late night at work and got a taxi back all the way to St Albans, crying.

However, once she woke up she started feeling much better. Part of what had been eating away at her was what a terrible shame it was, to throw away such a wonderful partnership. How in sync she had felt with Alex, how she'd felt as though he knew her deeply, in every corner of her soul. And yet, this man with whom she had apparently shared fifteen years of her life clearly did not know her at all. That, in a way, made it easier to let go of him. Her relationship had not been what she thought it was. It might not all have been a lie, but he certainly did not know her the way she felt he did. And, to be fair, vice versa. She had thought he would never want to be a father, and there he was, drunk, asking her if she would like to get pregnant. Clearly, they were not the match made in heaven they had thought they were.

Sarah was feeling more positive. She went jogging around St Albans and even enjoyed the occasional game of Hungry Hungry Hippos with her nieces. Not wanting children did not mean she couldn't enjoy their company, in small doses. She was finding her feet again. That's when the call from the estate agent came. Alex had loathed the man, and she could not blame him. He was sweaty and unpleasant, and always wore the most obnoxious ties. This time she liked him even less as he was bearing bad news. The buyers had definitely pulled out of the sale. In fact, apparently, they no longer wanted to move. This was distressing. The flat had to go back on the market.

It felt as though she had been set back by light years. All that paperwork, all for nothing. All that time, all for nothing. They would have to start again, with the viewings and the offers and eventually the various legal hoops to jump through before she could finally be free of the flat and all it represented. Since she had left, Sarah had been back a few times to pick up some clothes and she had found it heartbreaking. The apartment was not just the home she had shared with Alex, it was the symbol of their broken dreams. The thought of having to go back again and again to sell it was too much. It was depressing. It made her feel as though she was stuck in a field of quicksand, keeping her tethered to Alex even though he was a whole continent away. That is when Julia set her up on a date with Steve.

Steve was, in many ways, the opposite of Alex. He was a proper bloke, a guy's guy. A dude. He was loud and funny in an earnest way and knew about DIY and fixing cars. He had lived in Hong Kong for many years and had just come back to England. He did not know many people and was keen to make new friends. He enjoyed meeting new people, which was why he loved his job as a salesman so much. Alex would have secretly hated him. Nevertheless, Sarah agreed to go for one drink with him, because he was an old university friend of Julia's and she was asking so nicely. Also, Sarah needed a distraction from the real-estate disaster that was her flat.

They went to the All Bar One and had cocktails at happy hour, which was the sort of cheesy, vacuous thing her and Alex used to mock other people for. To her surprise, she had a nice time. Steve was funny and interesting and had plenty of travel stories from his years of selling security systems all over Asia. He was also very well read and very well travelled. Every year, he read all the books on the shortlist for the Man Booker prize. He had been to Antarctica. He liked to play and watch rugby, which was another thing her and Alex would have mocked him for. And yet, she liked him.

Cocktails turned into dinner at a Pizza Express, which turned into a steamy after-dinner at his tiny flat by the St Albans train station. Sarah could not quite believe it, as she took off her bra. She was in bed with a man, less than a month after breaking up with her long-term partner. What was happening to her?

The morning after was very much a surprise. She had expected to have to perform the Walk of Shame alone, sneaking into Julia's house without the children noticing. Instead, he'd made her eggs Benedict, and he'd driven her to Julia's so she could get changed before work. Once she got out of the house after a quick shower, she realised he was still there. To give her a lift to the station. He opened the car door for her. He was a gentleman, which was not something Sarah had ever thought she would appreciate in a man. And yet, as she sat on the train into work, she found herself smiling.

Inexplicably, they kept seeing each other. The places he took her were a Who's Who list of things that Alex and her London friends would find desperately uncool and depressing. They had dinner at Zizzi's, followed by a pint at the Green Giant pub down the road. They went to an AMC cinema to watch one of the Avengers movies, and he got her a Coke and sweet-and-salty popcorn. They went for a picnic in the park, which was all from Waitrose and very nicely packaged. The trouble was, those things were nice. Zizzi's pasta was unauthentic, but delicious. The Green Giant was friendly and spacious. Marvel films were entertaining, and Waitrose picnics were delicious. He took care of things for her. He made reservations, he came to pick her up.

Slowly yet steadily, Sarah found herself forgetting about her past. This new life was so nice, she could melt into it. When she had to cancel on him because of work, he understood. Sometimes, he would come to the office instead, with a picnic they ate in the hallway on those shiny designer chairs no one ever sat on.

Julia was ecstatic. "He's such a good guy," she would say, with a big smile, every time Sarah came back from one of their dates. "He's so funny, and clever, too!"

Sarah could not help herself but agree. He was funny and clever, although not in the way Alex had been funny and clever. She was getting used to it and had even watched half of a rugby match on a Sunday afternoon in the pub with Steve. Not because she now liked rugby, but because he did and he was just so nice.

He came round Julia's house for Sunday roasts, bringing a delicious dessert every time. He played with the children with unashamed delight, taking part in their games as if he were a child himself. He laughed at their jokes and spun them into the air like toy aeroplanes. Sarah's nieces adored him, and drew him stick-figure pictures that he oooh'd and aaaaah'd over like they were genuine pieces of art. He let the girls put make-up on him, and a *Frozen* wig that sat awkwardly on top of his mop of curly hair. He made no secret of adoring children, which Sarah found safer, in a way. He would not lie to her, to appease her for the time being hoping she may change her mind. Of course they didn't discuss kids – it was far too early in the relationship.

One day, as they were walking through Oxford Street (another place she would never, ever have gone with Alex but that was, secretly, fun), he gushed over a couple of small blond children running ahead of their mother, trailing behind laden with shopping bags.

"Ah, they're lovely," he said, with a big-kid grin. "I can't wait to have my own. I reckon, I'll have loads. How many children do you want?"

Sarah felt as though someone had slapped her in the face with a cold glove. He hadn't asked her whether she wanted kids, he had asked her how many. Implying she would want some. She knew exactly how to reply, and yet, for some reason, she didn't. She walked with him silently for a few seconds, thinking.

"I guess I've never really thought about that," she said slowly. And that was true. She had only ever thought about not having them at all. "I guess I would have two, so they can have each other when they grow older."

There was something about that image, the idea of two grown adults finding comfort in each other because they were raised together and loved by the same people, that made her want to cry. Having never desired kids, she had never stopped to consider what kind of people they would be like if she did.

Steve did not pick up on that. He moved on to talking about something else: clearly, for him that had been an off-the-cuff remark. How funny, how a casual comment from one person could change someone else's whole life. Sarah was quiet for the rest of the day.

Once they made it back home, she sat on her bed thinking. Maybe, just maybe, she could now see how other people came to start a family. She could imagine a life with Steve that was so clear she could see each step of it, like a ladder to normality. They would keep seeing each other for a few months. Then, he would ask her to move in with him to get away from her sister's place. Julia had been more than hospitable, but sooner or later things would get awkward. They would live together in the tiny flat by the station; Sarah would commute in every day, and she would find dinner ready on her return.

He would try to make up for the provinciality of it all by cooking fancy dinners: lemon sole with samphire, pork tenderloin with a plum sauce, home-made sushi. Eventually, he would propose somewhere dramatic, on a cliffside, perhaps, or, horrifyingly, on top of the Shard. They would get married somewhere lovely, with a church, and guests, and hats. She would get off birth control a few months later. She could see it all unfold, and for a few minutes she daydreamed about it actually happening. What used to terrify her now filled her with heart-warming familiarity. No shouting matches over the phone, no crying in taxi cabs on the way home from the airport. Just a simple happy life with mere touches of individuality.

If she could think of this life with Steve, she thought, didn't she owe it to Alex to give it a go with him first? She could be over in New York by dinner time tomorrow, she thought while getting into bed. If she could think of having real-life children with Steve, whom she barely knew, shouldn't she want to have children with Alex, whom she loved with all her heart? Right as she was starting to fall asleep, she texted him. *We need to talk*, she wrote rather dramatically. She slept poorly, and once she woke up she regretted it immediately. She knew the text was a mistake. It was too late. Even though it had only been a few short weeks, her and Alex had drifted apart in ways that could never be reconnected. What's more, Alex deserved someone who was actually excited about starting a family with him. What he did not deserve was her disrupting his new life, saying that maybe, potentially, one day she could see herself having two children. When he called her, she fudged a normal conversation, asking after his friends and new life. It was strange, she knew it, but it was too late to change course.

Perhaps this was not even about children. Every time she thought about having a family with Steve she could actually picture it, in a way that she never could with Alex. Steve would haul his children over his shoulders during rambunctious country walks, while Alex hated the country and had never been known to haul anything over his shoulders other than the occasional sandbag at the gym. Perhaps everyone else was right, it really was about Finding The Right Person all along. Perhaps it was just that as much as she loved Alex, he was not The One For Her. Maybe Steve was, which was why she could imagine being his wife, taking his shirts to be dry-cleaned and ironing his children's school uniforms. Maybe.

In the meantime, viewings for the flat were stacking up. It was a beautiful place, and people flocked to see it. They gushed over the view, over the open-plan living space and would make disappointed noises realising how small it was. She had taken to actually showing people around, hoping her presence would be less off-putting than that of the real estate agent, who was becoming cartoonishly more and more unpleasant with every visit. It was a cold Saturday morning in February when he called to say he had a couple interested in the place, and to ask whether she could come down that afternoon.

"These are cash buyers," he said. "And no chain."

To her eternal shame, she felt a shiver of excitement run down her spine. If they liked the place, this whole nightmare could be over in a few weeks. She could transfer Alex his half of the loot and then be free of his ghost forever. He could start his new life overseas and she could see if there really was such a thing as opposites attracting with Steve. Steve who was, at that moment, giving her a foot massage after she had tortured her feet in too-high boots all of Friday night. She was wearing one of his shirts, oversized, and running her fingers through his rebellious thick hair as he worked his way through the tense muscles on the soles of her feet. She was, in a very simplistic and animalistic way, very very happy. If she sold the flat, she could live here. Get her feet rubbed every day, and never think of Alex and his sad eyes again.

She hurried into London before lunch. She really wanted to make a good impression. She wore a simple calf-length black dress, with black suede boots and a cream-coloured silk scarf. She was wearing her camel overcoat, and had piled on the dark make-up on her eyes. On her way into the flat, she picked up two packets of red apples from the corner shop, and a bottle of orange juice. Once inside, she tumbled the apples in a matte ceramic bowl and strategically placed it on the countertop, with a glass decanter full of orange juice and four glasses. She had read a few blog posts on set design and knew that to entice people into a property you have to encourage them to picture themselves living there. Nothing does that as much as beautifully arranged food.

The couple were in their mid-sixties. They were both exceptionally well dressed and very well groomed. She sported a short dramatic haircut with an asymmetric fringe and an emerald-green scarf that made her eyes pop. He was wearing what was clearly a tailored suit, and a pocket square that matched his tie. They walked around the apartment and Sarah watched them fall in love with it. They reminded her of herself and Alex when they had come for their viewing, all those years earlier.

They were holding hands, and occasionally the man was running his hand across the woman's shoulders. They were excited about the view from the living room and loved the privacy of the bedroom. They were both enthusiastic about the walk-in shower and the underfloor heating. He made a slightly blue remark about the shower that made her blush and giggle, before she hurriedly told him off. They were rather oblivious to the presence of Sarah and that of the estate agent. Nevertheless, she offered them a glass of orange juice and they all stood around the narrow kitchen island, slowly sipping from their frosted glasses.

"How are you finding moving back to the UK?" the estate agent asked.

"It's been wonderful." The woman turned to Sarah. "We have lived in Berlin for the past few years, you see. We've come home for good, we think."

He let out a small chuckle. "I'm sorry." He playfully tugged on his wife's coat. "It's just that we have lived in a few places around the world. Singapore, Tokyo. New York, before that. She always thinks we're done, and then something else crops up."

"That's wonderful." Sarah really thought it was.

"Do you have kids, then?" The estate agent kept getting more and more irritating. If this couple didn't put in an offer, Sarah thought, she might fire him.

The couple shook their heads as they finished up their glasses.

"Not really for us, I'm afraid," he answered.

His wife gave him a big beaming smile and tousled his hair. They really did not seem to be able to keep their hands off each other.

Sarah froze, as the couple politely said their goodbyes and walked out, trailed by the estate agent in his garish tie and even more garish shirt. She stood there, feeling like a stranger in her own kitchen, still with her coat on, clutching her empty glass of juice. From the window she could see the reflection of the sun setting, the dull winter sky ablaze with pale shades of lemon yellow and light orange. Her eyes filled with tears, which rolled down her cheeks dragging long black marks along. She didn't sob or make a sound. She didn't wipe her eyes or try to stop crying. She just let her face become wetter and wetter with huge wobbling tears, as her make-up streaked all the way down to her chin.

She could play pretend with lovely Steve all day long. She knew what life she wanted, and she knew who she wanted to be when she turned sixty. She wanted to be shopping for cool flats in a great city, with a lifetime of adventures and travel behind her. She wanted to be in love, and she wanted to be free.

18

PAUL
RESOLUTION

The marquee fluttered gently in the summer breeze. The warm Kent sun was streaming through the kitchen window. Paul watched the clouds running across the sky. Only a couple were left, across the light blue sky.

"Lovely day for it, darling," his mum said as she came into the kitchen from the garden. She was holding an oversized bunch of daffodils in her hand. "These were behind the marquee. I thought we might as well have them in the house."

Paul went over and wrapped her in his arms. "Are you all right, Mum?" he asked gently.

"Ah I'm great. Thanks, love." She smiled widely. "It's just emotional, you know? My little boy, all grown up."

He didn't say anything, just gave her a big squeeze with his long arms. She pulled a tray of little tarts out of the fridge. Asparagus and goat's cheese, red onion chutney and butternut squash. She'd spent half the night making those. Paul suddenly realised he'd learned to show love through cooking from his mother.

"I think I'll just pop these under the grill for a few minutes before they start to arrive," she said, thoughtfully.

"Lucinda!" his dad called from outside. "Lucinda!" He was panicking. Dad always panicked when there was an event.

The marquee was set up right against the house, opening onto the dining room so people could move in and out through the open French doors. His dad was standing on a ladder, holding a tangled snake of white bunting.

"Lucinda," he said again. "I don't know how you want this. Do you want it across," he gestured, "or criss-cross?" He waved his arms expansively.

"Is that from Jim's wedding?" Paul asked. His brother had gotten married in his parents' garden five years before, and they still had all the decorations in the garage.

"Yes, Paul," his mum said distractedly. Then to his dad, on the ladder, "Just like we had it last time. Across the marquee."

"Aye," said his dad, "Of course. The harder way. Come and help me, son."

"Don't be ridiculous," she quipped right back. "Paul doesn't have time for this! He needs to go get ready!"

"Oh Mum, I do have time. It's only nine. Holly doesn't get here until eleven!"

"All right, dear, but do hurry." She scuttered away. His mother was a world-class party planner, she had things to do. And she loved a good marquee.

Paul climbed on the ladder on the opposite side to his dad's. He untangled the bunting, each little flag beating in the morning wind.

"How are you feeling, son?" God, he loved his parents. His dad defied every stereotype of the emotionally illiterate male and distant father. He had worked in the city for forty years, and had always made it back to Kent by the end of the day. Sometimes it was after Paul and his brothers had gone to bed, but he always made it back. He always had time to talk, even in the years when he was really busy and it was late at night, at the expense of his own sleep. While he had admittedly not done many loads of laundry or cooked many meals when Paul and his brothers were little, he had always more than pulled his weight emotionally.

"I'm good, Dad. In fact, I'm excited."

"Are you sure you want to do this? I'm only asking because it's all rather new." He seemed embarrassed. "Your mother and I don't want you to make hasty decisions in the heat of the moment."

"I know, Dad. But this is right for me right now."

"I trust you, son. And we love Holly!" He smiled. His dad found it easy to say nice things about people.

"I'm really happy about that. You've not had that much time together." Holly had only visited the house in Kent a handful of times since they'd got together.

"Love." His mum had crept back out behind him. "We've got more out of Holly in seven months than we did out of Alice in the decade you two were seeing each other." Mum had never liked Alice. She'd never said anything, of course, but she didn't have to. With Holly, he knew she meant it.

They finished setting up the bunting, and Paul sat there watching it wave in the breeze for a few minutes. His brothers, Jim and George, arrived and they all had a big cooked breakfast. Jim and his wife had come down from Glasgow on a morning flight, they were staying on for a whole week to catch up with English family and friends. Jim went on about his gap-year adventure in the Andes throughout breakfast. His wife affectionately ruffled his hair and joked he would no longer be allowed to just take off for a few months to the other side of the world. She was pregnant, only a few weeks along. Paul was the only other one who knew. "You'll miss the announcement," Jim had said, "but we still wanted to tell you in person. Please keep it a secret from Mum though!" Paul had a feeling Jim's wife didn't know that he knew. That could be a disaster waiting to happen. Didn't matter, he would not say a word.

After breakfast, Paul was shipped off to "get ready". How he was supposed to shower and dress for an hour and a half was unclear. He was in his room, looking over some of his old books, when he caught a glimpse of Holly getting out of her dad's car from the window. He smiled to himself. She'd promised him a surprise, and there it was. Her hair, a faded teal the last time he'd seen her, was a bright fuchsia colour. It moved loosely in the wind as she tried to keep the full skirt of her dress down. She was laughing, and she looked beautiful. He threw on his shirt and ran downstairs. They collided in the hallway, just as Holly was introducing her dad to his parents.

"Paul!" his mother squealed. "You're not wearing any trousers! Go put some on, immediately!"

His eyes met with Holly's. She looked so beautiful today, it was as though the sun was shining just on her face. She was laughing.

"All right, all right," he mumbled, and ran back up the stairs.

By the time he came back down, dressed in his finery, his parents had installed Holly, her mum and dad at the breakfast table. His brothers were standing around. Everyone held a glass of champagne in their hand. He checked nervously to see how Holly's parents were doing. "They get twitchy around your kind," she'd joked. She meant posh people. They seemed perfectly at ease. His parents were, all in all, good eggs. His mum especially could make anyone feel welcome in her home.

"Paul, well done, mate," said George. "We were about to have a toast. We probably won't get a chance later."

He shoved a glass in Paul's hand. It was chilled to perfection, and filled with bubbles up to the top.

"Right." His dad got up and raised his glass. "This is for my youngest son, Paul. Today, we are celebrating you setting off on a twelve-month adventure across the world with your wonderful girlfriend, Holly." He nodded in her direction and she raised her glass. "You leave tomorrow morning from London Gatwick a young man full of talent and you will hopefully return older, wiser and stronger than you were before." The room erupted in giggles. Holly and her parents clapped, and everyone clinked their glasses.

They still had an hour or so before guests would start to arrive. What had started off as a small gathering had snowballed into quite a medium-sized one. All their friends from London were coming down, and everyone in his large family wanted to come along and wish him bon voyage. They were going to Southeast Asia first. Thailand, then Cambodia. They planned to take the train through Vietnam. Then Indonesia, then Fiji. Then South America, probably. Mexico, perhaps, or maybe Peru. The trip of a lifetime. They had plans to stop for a few weeks in a couple of places, and work remotely doing copy editing to earn some money. The work was boring and not particularly well paid, but it would get them far in not depleting their budget too quickly.

They strolled to the bottom of the garden and sat on the crumbling set of swings his parents were still holding on to in the hope of grandchildren. Boy, were they going to be happy once they heard Jim's news.

"Are you happy?" Holly asked. The sunlight shone through the first leaves on the trees, throwing angular patterns on the cream skirt of her dress. He recognised it as one of her granny's, something she would have worn as a much younger woman.

"I am so happy I can barely breathe," he replied.

They sat on the swings for a while, looking back at the house where preparations were in full swing. Holly's dad had been roped in to help set up the barbeque. Paul's mind drifted back, to the last time he'd sat in the garden.

❦

It was much colder. It was the middle of autumn, and fog was rising from the ground like smoke. He had just got home from his wonderful and devastating time in Essex. Brown dead leaves were falling off the trees. The countryside smelled like home. His mother had demanded he shower, dress and get out of the house for at least an hour. She had meant for him to go for a walk, but he was taking a perverse pleasure in defying her wishes. He'd sat on the cold hard ground. It had been drizzling all day, and the grass was wet. His jacket was too big for him: in the last three weeks since he'd arrived home, in the middle of the night, he had barely eaten anything. He'd lost weight and his hair was flopping in front of his eyes like a mop. He didn't shave either, and was growing a terrifying wispy thing on his upper lip. He took out his phone and started fidgeting with it. He went on Facebook, scrolling through aimlessly. Then, he got a terrible idea. He relished how bad this was going to be for him. He found Alice and hovered with his thumb over the "Unblock" button. It had been over three years now. God knows how much he had to catch up on. He would have a look at what she was up to, see how much fun she was having travelling, yet another woman – like Holly – who preferred taking selfies on the beach to sitting at home with him. What he saw felt like a punch in the gut.

Alice was pregnant. Not just that, she was married. There were wedding photos, all her friends dressed up as bridesmaids, their peach-coloured dresses swirling as they danced. From what he could make out, the wedding was somewhere in Australia. Somewhere indoors, very traditional looking. She'd been wearing a big poofy tulle dress that was everything she'd said she didn't want. It looked like they had gone to Sydney for a short honeymoon, which was a far cry from her notions of long travels in remote places. That was almost two years earlier. Now she was just a woman who lived with her husband in a lovely little town-home in suburban Melbourne.

She posted photos of the two of them having brunch on the balcony, squeezed on a tiny round table amongst the red geraniums they kept in the window boxes. There were pictures of them repainting the kitchen, from an outdated yellow to a classy muted green. There were pictures of the two of them cooking together in their newly repainted kitchen. Pictures of her shopping with her friends for nursery decor. Pictures of her baby shower, where she sat, radiant, as she unboxed little shoes, toys and baby books. He could not begin to comprehend it.

He scrolled back, looking for pictures of her travels. There were none. If her Facebook timeline was to be believed, she'd moved to Australia, got a job, had one short holiday back to England for Christmas and then just started her new life right there in Melbourne. She'd made new friends, went on nights out clubbing and to fancy bottomless brunches. She'd fallen in love with a new friend from the gym. She had never gone to the gym while they were together, but she had seemingly taken up some serious exercise since moving down under. There were pictures of her at Zumba class, sharing a green smoothie with friends after yoga and going for long runs on the harbour.

Who was this woman, living in Alice's skin? She looked the same. But couldn't be the same. This woman liked to cook and took days off to have staycations with her husband where they watched old movies and ate ice cream. This woman was having a baby. What's the difference, he wondered, between this and what we would have had? He felt betrayed, while at the same time feeling relieved. He really was over her. He wasn't jealous, he didn't want her for himself. But he was confused. She'd uprooted her life, just to go live the same life on the other side of the world with some guy she hadn't yet met. Paul could see himself spiral towards a new fixation. Understanding Alice; something he thought he'd never care about again.

After an indefinite period of time, his dad came out of the house. He was holding an umbrella and stood over him. Paul hadn't realised it was raining.

"Hey, son," he said.

"Can you sit down, Dad?"

His father sat. He was wearing beautiful brown corduroys, and he was probably very upset about having to cover them with mud. But he sat down anyways. He was a good dad.

Paul told him. He told him everything, even things he'd not told his mother in their long heart-to-heart the night he got home. He told his dad about Holly, about how betrayed he felt. About how he thought every woman in the world would prefer to go somewhere with palm trees rather than love him. He told him about Alice, and how she was now living their life with a better-looking guy somewhere warmer. His father listened, his eyes closed, under the big umbrella. The rain got to be pretty heavy, but neither of them moved. After Paul was finished talking, they sat there in silence, listening to the rain. It was oddly comforting, even though Paul's legs were wet.

Paul's dad had shaken his head.

"Paul," he'd said, with a deep shrug, "I don't know what to tell you. When I was young, before I met your mother, I had no interest in settling down and having children." Paul frowned. Imagining his dad not being a dad had always seemed like a slightly impossible feat. He was, and had always been, a dad. He'd seen photos of him when he was younger, of course, but it all seemed slightly made-up.

"I was living in London," his dad continued, "and loving every minute of it. We're talking about the eighties here, son. That was the time to be in London. The parties, the girls. It was crazy."

"Dad, please don't talk about cocaine."

"Who said anything about cocaine? It was good clean family fun. I even had a girlfriend there, for a while. And she was always unhappy, because I didn't want to propose, and I didn't want to get married. We even lived together for a few months."

"You had a live-in girlfriend before Mum?" That was out of this world. "Does she know?"

His father laughed. He didn't often chuckle, but this time he was really amused. "Of course your mother knows! She was there!"

"Hang on, what?"

"For goodness' sake, Paul, I thought you were a man of the world. Your mother and I met when I was going out with this other girl and, well, we fell in love. I moved out immediately."

Paul let out an audible gasp. He didn't want to hear that. It was too personal, like seeing his dad naked. No reason he shouldn't know but still, not what he wanted to hear. His father continued, getting to the point. "And suddenly I was the one trying to convince your mother to marry me. I proposed twice before she listened to me. She wanted to live in Kent, and after we spent an afternoon here I was on board. My old girlfriend must have mentioned moving out of London maybe a hundred times and I kept pretending I didn't get the hint. I got it all right."

Paul looked at his dad with fresh eyes. He had never thought of him that way, like a man who had made a set of decisions that had led, eventually, to him being his dad.

He carried on. "And I wanted to have her babies pretty quickly after that. I'm not kidding, your brother, Jim, was mostly my idea."

"Dad, please." Paul wrinkled his nose.

"Why does every generation always think they've invented sex?"

"Dad, please."

"Right, whatever. We found the three of you on the roof, after the stork had been by. My point is, the life I was dreading with my old girlfriend was, well, paradise with your mother. For almost forty years."

"But why?"

"You see, son." His dad got up and shook off his sodden muddy trousers. "It's not so much about what you do in life. It's who you do it with."

Paul sat on the grass for a while longer. At lunchtime, his mum brought him a cheese toastie and a cup of tea. He got up, and actually went for a long walk, all the way to the other side of the village. Then he came home and sat up with his parents to watch *Masterchef*. The following morning, he shaved and showered properly for the first time in a while. He put a change of clothes in his old school backpack, which was still hanging in his bedroom, and left for the train station. He didn't need much. He still had plenty of clothes at Holly's, if she would take him back. The rain had stopped, and the sun was peeking through the dark clouds. There might as well be a rainbow, he thought.

And there he was, seven months later. Waiting for his own farewell party to start. He held Holly's hand as they both swung in unison, looking up at the light blue sky. For the first time in his life, he couldn't picture a single stitch of his future. He smiled.

19

FLORENCE

Florence called out to Spencer. He came through, holding his leash in his mouth. A cute trick she'd taught him, to make sure she could always find the leash. His training had come such a long way since the move. Florence stepped out into the cold morning air. The spring sky was clear, the light cutting right through the bare branches of the trees, barely covered with new buds. While her family in London was sending her pictures of daffodils in flower, spring was lagging slightly behind in Scotland. She had been delighted to discover that her front garden was laden with snowdrops. But spring was certainly in the air this morning. The grass was green, and shining with morning dew. A single prune tree was covered in tiny white blossoms. She looked over, to the hills of Fife.

She pushed off the jogging stroller. Inside, Tim was cradling Miriam. She was asleep, enjoying her morning nap with a slight smile on her face. Both children were wrapped up warm in giant hand-knitted hats. She started running, first gently and then at a faster pace up the lane, away from the village. Spencer kept up, with huge leaps and bounds. His tongue was lolling out of his mouth, his eyes lit with excitement. That was a happy dog, if ever there was one. They reached the main path, and ventured into the woods. The naked branches of the trees let in all the rays of the sun, but it was still chilly. Florence was thankful for her own bobble hat, and for her thermal leggings.

Tim waved frantically at his furry best friend through the stroller window. He had come such a long way too since they'd moved. He was going to a lovely childminder's three days a week, and he had learnt so many new things. He could count, point out colours and animals. He had made little friends, whose mums Florence was slowly but steadily befriending. They'd had coffees at the local pub, and even the occasional wine night in. She missed her friends in London, of course, but she already felt very much at home in Scotland. While she'd never lived anywhere but London, she used to spend long summer holidays at her grandparents' house in Perthshire and she had always felt a true fondness for the place. She loved living in a small village, where everybody knew everybody and she could leave the back door unlocked (not that she ever did, she was still a city girl at heart). She also loved being so close to Edinburgh, less than an hour if the traffic was good. Every Tuesday morning she got in her tiny third-hand car and drove into town to go to the office. It had been so long since she last had an office to go to, she still felt as though every Tuesday was a little holiday.

They reached the top of the hill, and Florence turned round to take in the view of the village, nestled amongst the muddy fields. Little clouds of smoke were rising from people's chimneys. A few people were out and about with their dogs. She took in a big breath of chilly morning air, and started stretching.

"This was a good idea," she said quietly to herself. It was her morning ritual: the run, the stretches, the affirmation. "This was a good idea," she'd said that first morning, when she'd felt so overwhelmed with the house full of boxes, Tim crying, Spencer barking and Miriam, only eight weeks old, staring at her from her Moses basket. It had quickly become apparent it had, in fact, been a great idea.

20

FLORENCE

It all started one calm afternoon, three days before her due date when she was very ready for her pregnancy to be over. They'd moved to her parents' house almost immediately after she'd heard about John. In fact, they had gone over as soon as they'd heard the news, and they had never really moved back. The tiny pink house with its crown of wisteria was no longer the house of her dreams, Florence had quickly realised. It was beautiful, but it was too intrinsically linked to John in her mind for her to be able to ever enjoy living there again. It was where they'd been happy. It was where they'd first brought Tim home from the hospital. It was where she'd found out John had been cheating on her with the receptionist. It was where she'd told him to leave. It was where she was standing, frozen in horror, when the phone had rung and she'd found out John was dead.

A drug overdose, which was ridiculous because John had never done drugs, not even at university. And yet, there it was. They had found him in his little bedsit, after he failed to show up for work for two days in a row. It had taken two days for them to think something was wrong. Apparently he had been in trouble with his boss, and they all thought he was hiding out for fear of getting fired. The whole story was impossible, unbelievable, like his affair, and yet, like his affair, it was definitely true.

The words from the kind police detective over the telephone felt like a punch in the gut. She had hated John so much, but all she wanted was to get him back. Florence would never want to erase John from her life. He was Tim and Miriam's father. She had very much loved him for a very long time. After she hung up the phone, all she wanted to do was run home. She knew she needed a fresh start. Also, she was about to have a baby. She'd packed up and moved in with her parents. Adapting to a dog and a toddler living in the house had been a challenge for them, but they had been wonderful and very supportive.

That fateful afternoon, Florence was sat on the sofa enjoying a restful cup of tea. Her mum had taken Tim out for a walk to feed the ducks in the park. She was browsing wallpaper for the new baby's room. Tim was still sleeping with her, but she would try to get Miriam to sleep in her own room as soon as she could. Things would be different this time around. Miriam could go in the study, it had been decided. It was barely even used anymore, and it was right next door to her own room. So Florence was browsing for children's wallpaper. Little pink flowers. Little ducks. A whole zoo of animals wearing tiny hats, in a Mardi Gras procession. That one was cute, and Miriam would probably enjoy it even when she grew up. And then it hit her. She was planning to stay at her parents' house forever. She was getting wallpaper that her child would enjoy six, seven years down the line. She would be that woman, whose life had failed so miserably she and her children had to live with her parents. That woman whose life had been cancelled. People would ask after her with a genuine note of concern in their voice. Her parents would never stop treating her like a child herself. They would share in the burdens and responsibilities of raising her children. Motherhood would be easy from now on, when she could split it three ways.

For the first time in many years, Florence felt a motion of rebellion stir up inside her. This life did not belong to her. This was not what she was looking for. Living with her parents was the done thing, what was expected of a young widow of thirty-two with very little work experience and two small children. But she had done what was expected all her life, and it had not been going well for her. She should try something different.

She scrolled back on her phone, to her Instagram account. It was not something she had ever thought of as an accomplishment, but it was, by most people's standards, quite impressive. She had over thirty thousand followers, tuning in every day to her carefully manicured selections of photos of everyday life. Instagram had been, for a long time, her only artistic outlet. Even in her busiest and most desperate days of early motherhood, she found a few minutes to take a picture of something beautiful every few days, edit it to match her style and share it with the world. People seemed to respond. She had never thought of making money from it. Could she even do that? Maybe, but probably not to make a living. Be real, Florence, she told herself. Being an Instagram influencer is not a real job. Not for you, anyways.

She clicked on the pulsating icon at the top of her screen. It was a new story, from a homewares and interior decor brand she loved. It was called Polka Dots, and she owned almost every single one of their bakeware items. She had been following them on Instagram for years, just to fill her feed with beautiful images of rustic decor. They had followed her back, and they enjoyed regular chit-chat on a variety of weighty subjects, such as which colour peonies would look best in her new cream vase. They were virtual friends, her and Polka Dots, in one of those bizarre interactions that made her feel like she was truly a participant in the modern day. The story that popped up on the screen was different from their everyday content. They posted mostly photos of their products, and other action shots of life in the Scottish countryside. This one was just plain text, on a pale green background. It made Florence sit up and read it over.

They were looking for a new part-time social media manager. The person currently looking after the account was moving on, and they needed someone to replace her. Could this be a sign? It was absurd, Florence told herself. For one, she didn't have any qualifications. New media was a subject you could get a degree in, and you presumably needed one to become the social media manager of a well-known brand. Secondly, she had no experience. And crucially, this job would be somewhere remote in the Scottish countryside, even though flexible working was encouraged.

Turns out it was actually in Edinburgh. She found this out when, after sending her CV and a one-page letter she did not read back for spellcheck, she heard back from them wanting to arrange an interview. An interview in Edinburgh. While the vibe of the brand was very country-like, they explained, the actual office was in Edinburgh. This was crazy, she thought. Impossible. She was two days overdue at that point, there was no way she could get on a train to Edinburgh. And yet, bizarrely, she did. She got up before dawn, took a taxi to the station and was on the first fast train out. She made it in time for her interview, which went well. They knew her from her Instagram account of course.

She was nervous as she pitched her idea, which she had only fully formed on the train up. She had once heard that J. K. Rowling had come up with the concept for Harry Potter on a train to Scotland. It must have been an inspiring train ride, because here was her own breakthrough. The idea was simple. She would purchase a real-life model home, a cottage perhaps, somewhere in the countryside near Edinburgh. Polka Dots would furnish it with vintage pieces and, wherever possible, Polka Dots wares. There would be thick ceiling beams strung with hand-sewn pastel bunting, a wall piano, a small cream-coloured Aga in the kitchen. She would make the whole cottage a living photography set for Polka Dots wares. Keep it as on-brand as possible.

She would move in, with her children, and live life as it came. She would take photos, and document their lives. She would share them on social media. People would want to live her life and would buy the stuff. Of course, she would still do all the other things a social media manager is meant to do: source influencers, respond to comments, make campaigns for year-round events. Promote new lines and launches. She knew what those things were, because she had googled them on her phone on the train ride up.

They didn't say much, but were very nice and bought her lunch. She worried she had embarrassed herself, but there was something comforting about embarrassing yourself so far away from home. She would never see these people ever again. She hadn't even told her parents she was going to a job interview, they thought she was with a friend. She got back on the train, and was somewhere unspecified in the middle of England when her phone rang. They didn't even want to interview anyone else, they said. When could she start? After speaking with them, Florence hung up the phone and spent the rest of the journey with her head tilted back and her eyes closed.

Once the train pulled into King's Cross, she got off and walked straight into a taxi. She gave him the address of Chelsea and Westminster Hospital, and rang her mum on the way. She asked her to meet her at the hospital bring her bag: she was going to stay overnight.

It wasn't until after Miriam was born that she'd had the

courage to tell them she was moving. She was worried they would be angry, like a teenager who wants to move in with her boyfriend and knows her parents will say no. Instead, they just seemed worried.

"How are you going to do this by yourself?" her dad asked, raising his eyebrow. It occurred to her that they might not be taking her seriously.

"The job is part-time, I'll work from home two out of the three days and the one day I have to go in I'll figure something out." She had felt really insecure about this plan. She didn't know if it was doable, and didn't know if she could do it. She was trying to convince her parents this was a good idea; she was somehow convincing herself too.

"You'll have no support!" chimed in her mother. She was definitely taking her seriously, and her carefully made-up face was contorted in a very worried expression.

Florence really thought about it for a second. She'd had all the support in the world with her first child: family close by, two grandmothers ready to come over at the ring of a mobile phone, lots of friends, a postpartum doula, endless baby groups and support groups. She'd still struggled. In fact, she'd found it all rather suffocating, an endless list of places she had to go to, to open up and be vulnerable. It was emotionally stressful, and actually took up quite a bit of her time. She was wary of sounding ungrateful, but that's just how she felt.

"Well, Mum," she said, hoping to avoid an argument, "I'll need to see how it goes."

That had been the key phrase: see how it goes. Convincing her parents this was some temporary fancy had allowed her to get their support enough to set the wheels in motion. The gods seemed to smile on her endeavour. She found a perfect cottage within a few weeks, doing most of the house-hunting on a smartphone in the middle of the night, while nursing her daughter. Her new colleagues were all but too happy to go and view it for her. They video called her during the viewing, and she felt they were already friends. These people were artsy, and mumsy. They were excited about the beautiful wooden beams that criss-crossed the ceilings, and the fireplace in original brick. So was she. In fact, she even felt her eyes getting moist, a tear lurking at the back of her throat, as she saw them run through the garden.

"You'll love this, Florence!" one of them screamed in the sunshine of that cold winter afternoon.

"Call me Flo," she replied with a smile. Her mother, from the other side of the room, raised an eyebrow. Nobody had ever called her that before.

Her father's last objection had been cost. Would she be able to afford it? Miraculously, she could. She'd called the estate agent the afternoon she'd moved back in with her parents after John's death, to see if they could still sell the house. Unfortunately their original buyer was no longer interested. Fair enough, he was probably buying a house somewhere else. The estate agent had seemed happy to hear from her though. He had just had a phone call from someone who might be perfect.

Florence had gone back to her old house one afternoon before a job at Polka Dots was even on her radar, to let the potential buyers in for a viewing. She was deeply ashamed, the house was a mess. She had not taken the time to clean or tidy before leaving; she had packed Tim and the dog in her dad's car and she had not looked back. And yet, the young couple looking at the house seemed to love it. They didn't even notice the splatter patterns on the kitchen backsplash, and didn't care about the stacks of old toys in the corner of the living room. They marvelled excitedly at the size of the tiny conservatory.

"It's a greenhouse!" the husband had exclaimed.

"We have a lot of plants," the wife had whispered, with a knowing smile.

Go figure. That's what it was. It wasn't a conservatory, of course. It was a greenhouse, an extravagance built by someone who wanted a hot place to grow mandarin oranges and tomatoes. How had they never figured it out? Florence had let out a half smile, thinking of poor John valiantly cramming his large body into that tiny space, aiming to work on his laptop precariously perched on an old card table. Even after all that had happened, that memory still made her smile. It had been a happy house. They had been happy there.

After only three days, the couple had put in an offer. It was lower than the asking price, and her father had urged her to play hardball. She refused. She could picture them, living happily in her tiny pink house. They would fill the greenhouse with luscious dark-green plants. Florence imagined a whole bookcase filled with beautiful pink orchids. As it turns out, the equity she had released from the house would more than cover the purchase of the cottage, with quite a bit left over. "London property prices are out of control," said her new colleagues over the phone. "Crazy. They make you lose all sense of proportion."

And just like that, it was time to leave. Her parents seemed to have slowly turned off their objections. Her mum was going to come up for a few weeks and help her get settled, but Florence had gone ahead with Tim and Miriam. They had shipped most of their things ahead, and Florence drove up in her new second-hand car. It was a long and exhausting journey. By the time they turned the key in the creaky door, the cottage was dark. It smelled damp and looked like a maze of boxes shut together with tape, a frightening forest of shadows. The downstairs lights did not seem to be working, so they went straight to bed upstairs. As she lay on the double bed with Tim and Miriam, Spencer snoring at the foot of the bed, Florence stared at the ceiling and cried silently. She was a long way from home, and all alone.

&.

In the morning, however, things seemed very different. She woke up around six, the first cold light of the street lamp flooding the room. There were no curtains. She got up, careful not to wake her children, and tiptoed downstairs. She took a drink of water from the large farmhouse-style sink, and walked around the rooms as the sun rose slowly, filling her new home with light. It felt like the good old days, when she had just moved to her little pink house and she would roam its rooms in the early morning, planning the redecoration. The cottage was a mess, furniture amassed against the walls and precarious-looking towers of cardboard boxes standing in her way.

But Florence could see past the mess. She could see the view from the kitchen window, a perfectly-framed vista of a beautiful ash tree. She could see the furniture her new employers had sent her, and it was beautiful. She started rearranging it in her mind. One piece in particular had caught her eye: a refurbished wall unit, painted in a dove grey. She could do something special with that.

What occurred to her immediately after was that arranging her new furniture was, technically speaking, part of her job. For the first time in years, she was excited about work. She should also buy some new clothes, something she liked herself in. With her second pregnancy, she had rid herself of all her pre-motherhood clothes and now she regretted it bitterly. Some of them would have reminded her of John, but she loved so many of her old pieces. She used to have a black-and-white houndstooth skirt she would have loved to still have, to wear to work with a black satin blouse and her old over-the-knee suede boots. Her new clothes would have to be from a charity shop, she could not justify buying new things she didn't really need.

Her life was changing, and in many ways it was going to be worse. Her new life as the happy single mother of two would feature far fewer luxuries than her old life as the unhappy married mother of one. No holidays for a while, probably, unless it was a treat from her parents. The children would go to state schools instead of the posh private place John had found near their would-be new home in Surrey.

John's family had offered to contribute, but she had chosen not to accept. No strings attached. They were welcome to visit any time, she'd told them, and she'd meant it. They were nice, and Tim loved his grandma. But this was going to be a new chapter in her life and Florence wanted to start it without John, or his ghosts. Her new job would pay enough for her and her children to live on, considering she had no mortgage. In four years' time, Miriam would go to school and Florence might switch to full-time. Who knows.

In the corner of the kitchen, she found a travel tea kettle. It came with two green plastic mugs, a box of teabags, two instant coffee pouches and two little long-life milk cartons. The previous owners must have left it for her when they moved her things in. So considerate. That would never happen in London. She made herself a tea and went to sit on her front step, cradling her mug with both hands. It was so cold outside, the mug steamed up with thick coils of vapour. She took in the first delicious sip and savoured it as she contemplated the view from her front door. She could see the whole village on one side, and a coiling lane going uphill, towards the woods. She should go up there for a run every morning, she thought, taking her second sip of tea. She savoured the quiet of the village waking up in the thick winter mist.

"Mummy!" Tim screamed from upstairs. She smiled. No

matter where she was, or who she was now, she was still Mummy.

"I'm coming, my love!" she hollered back.

As she got up from the doorstep, she took one last look at her new life. It was beautiful.

21

CLAIRE

Her children came in the night, one by one, as if answering a summons. She saw them pull up on the driveway, turn off the headlights and scuttle away from the house. She imagined they were all meeting somewhere in the village, probably the pub. They walked quickly, their hands deep in their pockets, their heads held low. They all lived busy lives, and yet they had all come. They had stopped whatever they were doing, halfway through their family suppers, school play rehearsals and their weekend plans. Like workers in a strike, they had downed tools to come here, quickly, steadily, in the night. It suddenly hit her that her sons were four men, grown and tall and prickly with an end-of-the-day stubble as they sat around a table, talking with hushed voices and worried faces. Her eyes blinked away a tear. She was so proud of her children, even when they broke her heart.

They came by the house at breakfast time, looking like they had all slept uncomfortably. Their shirts were wrinkled, they had not shaved. They looked like they might not have even showered. If, as she suspected, they had slept in the rooms above the local pub she was not surprised. They all sat around the kitchen table, their hands nervously running over the worn-down Formica top. Michael fussed about, getting cups of tea for everyone.

Jacob cleared his throat. He was clearly the one in charge. Claire could not help but smile. Jacob. Her big boy. He had always been the leader, in charge of their little tribe of feral boys. Aaron was the instigator, Jacob was the one making sure things didn't get out of hand. When Michael had been shot, Jacob was barely ten. He had looked after his brothers almost entirely on his own while Claire tried to piece together what had happened and then later, while she was nursing Michael back to health. She could see how this had shaped Jacob, from a determined little boy into a serious teenager and the man he had become. He was a wonderful father, a caring husband and highly respected in his profession. To Claire, he would always be the leader of her little pack of boys, four worried little faces peering through the door as she tried to help Michael to the bedpan.

They seemed much the same now as they had back then: Aaron bashful, Elijah wide-eyed and Gideon frightened, as they all looked to Jacob awaiting instructions, like little soldiers. He gestured with his hand, an encouraging smile on his face.

"I don't even know what to say." Aaron's voice was hoarse from crying. "Mum, I would be heartbroken if you thought even for a second that I meant what I said. Of course I don't, I have always admired you and Dad, now more than ever. I don't even know how you coped with the loss of a child the way you did."

Claire smiled. Her eyes were still full of tears. "We did it for you boys, you know? To give you a sense of normality."

Michael said something, and even Claire couldn't understand him. He had been up all night, and with his cracked voice it was impossible to distinguish any words. He shrugged with a smile and put his arm around her shoulders, gently pulling her towards him.

"This has been the worst year of my life," Aaron continued, "and things with Penelope have been so bad for so long, I was just looking for someone else to shout at." His head lolled forward, his lower lip protruding like a child doing an exaggerated expression of sadness.

Claire reached over the tabletop and clasped his hands in hers. "Darling," she said, softly, "I know. That's okay. And I know you didn't mean it."

"And I know you did it for us," Aaron said, looking back up again. "You did it to give us a normal childhood and a normal life and look, we spoke yesterday and one thing we are all agreed on is that we all really really appreciate it."

Jacob put his hand on Claire's arm. "It meant a lot to us, Mum," he said, softly.

Michael got up and opened his arms. Aaron rushed into them like he did when he was a little boy. Claire hugged him from behind, like a sandwich of parental love.

"Oh, I want a hug now!" Gideon, her baby, was trying to lighten the mood.

"Go on, then," said Claire with a giggle. "Pile on."

They all squeezed each other in a big family hug, arms weaving through arms, hands pushing down on backs. This was easier when they were little, thought Claire, but it sure feels nice now they are all grown.

"Right, now, Mum." Jacob untangled himself. "And Dad. There's something else we need to talk about."

The boys' faces dropped, as they all sat around the table.

"Is the apartment in Canary Wharf gone?" asked Jacob.

"Not yet," Claire replied. "We told them we were looking for another buyer. They said they would give us a month and then put it back on the market, so it's there waiting for us. Why?"

Elijah spoke for the first time, his voice cautious. "We think you deserve to get on with your lives. And we thought we could buy the house off you. The four of us, together, so you get to move on."

"Hang on, what?" Michael was confused, and so was Claire.

"We can do it up and sell it," Jacob explained, while cleaning his glasses with the front tails of his shirt. "Which would actually be an investment opportunity for us. Aaron could stay here for a while and help out with the renovations. But we could buy it off you first, so you don't lose your flat."

"How would you even afford it?"

"Mum, you'll be surprised to know some of us actually have quite good jobs," Gideon said with a smile that was also a smirk. There was always a little tension with Gideon. He felt as though he had to prove himself, the youngest of a brood of impressive men.

"This is Gideon's way of telling us his book is selling well." Elijah came right back at him. He would step into the role of class clown when Gideon was unavailable. Also, he was right, Gideon's book was selling well. He had written it in his spare evenings and weekends, edited it, proofread it, found an agent for it and sold it without saying a word to his mother. Claire's books had sold millions of copies and had been translated into five languages, and yet her son had not felt the need to tell her he was writing a book. She knew she had no right to be angry about that. As a journalist, he had plenty of good material. Most importantly, he was forging his own path. He didn't want to succeed because he was her son, he wanted to succeed because his book was interesting and well-written. Still, every time it was mentioned Claire felt a twinge of something resembling disappointment.

They all laughed at Elijah's quip. Michael raised his hand. "We know you are, but this is still quite a lot of money."

"Dad, for what this house will be worth after we renovate it, it will be a steal." Gideon was excited.

"And what about Aaron's refuge? What's happening with that?" Claire asked.

"Mum," he replied slowly, "I don't think it is going to work out."

"What did Penelope say?" Claire immediately regretted speaking her name.

Aaron took a big sigh, his shoulders slumping. "We realised that we can't open a charity together and get a divorce at the same time. We would both rather have the charity, but we very much need a divorce."

Claire put her hand on his shoulder. "Darling, are you sure about that? Is there nothing you can do?"

"Do you know," he replied, pulling himself up, "I genuinely thought, for a while, that we could patch things up. Have a common project to work on, be a team against all odds once again. The refuge was already pulling us together, in a way." Elijah got up and slumped his arms around Aaron's shoulders.

"But it's like Pandora's box, you know?" he continued. "Once you let it all out, you can't put it back in."

"Oh, Aaron, I'm so sorry." Claire could feel tears pooling at the back of her throat. No matter how old and wise her children became, they would always be her babies.

"That's okay, Mum," he replied quietly. "I think one way or another, we've always had it coming."

"It's so awful. I think the idea of the refuge was fantastic, and I think you would be so suited for that type of work." She sniffed loudly, trying to contain herself. This was no time to cry.

Jacob got up and moved towards the back wall of the kitchen, which featured four large corkboards. Claire had used them to help Aaron and Penelope set up the refuge and it was covered in a web of pinned papers, photographs and scribbled Post-it notes. In no official capacity, she and Michael had put in their fair share of hours helping develop a plan for the refuge, running ideas by Penelope as she came to visit. Jacob took his time, surveying the boards. Claire had not been able to bring herself to take them down, even now she knew the whole idea would never become reality.

Finally, Jacob turned round. "Dad, would you be sad about missing out on your new flat?"

Michael let out an audible snort. "This is funny. I asked the same exact question to your mother the other day."

Michael and Jacob turned towards her. She shook her head. "I guess neither of us was really too excited about moving. We love this house and..." she cleared her throat, "the only reason we are moving in the first place is that it's impractical for two people to live in a five-bedroom house."

Elijah raised an eyebrow. "So you didn't like your new place?" He sounded surprised. "But you said you loved it!"

"Well," Claire replied, slowly, "we did love it at the time. But I guess at least for me, I loved it the way you love a hotel room. It's nice, but I don't know if I would love living there."

"I think your mum is right." Michael put his hand on the back of her chair. "We did love it then. But then we realised we were not that upset about the idea of losing it."

"To be fair, Dad, it sounds like the only thing you are really upset about is the refuge." Gideon had his own, journalistic, way of surgically cutting through all the nonsense.

"You're right, love," whispered Claire. She was no longer going to cry, she just felt really sad.

They all sat in silence for a few minutes. The sun was

coming up, filling the kitchen with a faded winter light. The only sounds were the chattering of the birds outside, and the soft clinking of the tea mugs on the kitchen table.

"Mum," Aaron said suddenly. "I know this is weird, but hear me out."

22

CLAIRE

It was summer again. The garden had blossomed and was filled with light and the heady scent of freshly-cut grass. It would be time for lunch soon. Claire walked in from the garden carrying a large basket filled with green beans from her vegetable patch. She looked at the clock. Michael and the kids would be home in half an hour, she had to get a move on. If lunch wasn't ready by the time they got back, there would be hell to pay. She pulled out a large bowl of hard-boiled eggs from the fridge. They were raising chickens again, and always had more eggs than they knew what to do with. So that, she thought, was to be lunch. Hard-boiled eggs, steamed green beans and those two loaves of bread she had picked up from the bakery in the morning. There were pears for dessert, and she could make a quick custard to go with it.

As she hurried around in the kitchen, Aaron walked in. He was wearing his work clothes: a light pink shirt, and dusty blue chinos. A braided belt. Turns out, he cleaned up pretty nicely; now that he worked for MSF at their London offices, he had to.

"I'll go right after lunch," he said. "Would you like anything from London?"

"I think we're okay. Thanks, love." Claire smiled. "When are we expecting you back?"

"Oh it'll be quick, I only have a couple of meetings today and one tomorrow morning. And that's it for the week, I don't have to go in until Tuesday."

"That's nice." Claire had to raise her voice over the sound of the tap filling the steamer.

"I'm staying with Elijah, we might even go to the pub after dinner."

She smiled even wider. That was good. Since he'd made the move down to Surrey, only sporadically commuting up to London, Aaron was starting to heal. He was getting out, going to the pub or out to dinner with his brothers and old friends. No dates yet, but that was probably too early. Penelope had left King's Hospital to return to the Middle East, and their divorce was looking relatively straightforward. Still, it was awful even to think about. But Aaron seemed to be doing better and better.

"Where's Dad?" he asked.

"He's gone to the allotment with the kids," she replied, pouring the green beans in the steamer.

In addition to the back-garden vegetable patch, they had an allotment. Every day in the summer, the children would spend long hours there gardening. As well as weeding and pruning, they ran around chasing each other with the water hose, giggling in excitement. They had only been with them a few months, but they had already formed a tight pack, an indivisible unit. They all attended the local school together, the same school where Claire's children had gone.

They all played together and they even slept together. The big knocked-through bedroom her boys had asked for when they were younger had been turned into a dormitory-style space with four bunk beds. Aaron now lived in the old guest room, and they had converted the loft into a large light-filled playroom.

The last remaining room, which had, for the longest time, stored boxes and old exercise equipment, was occupied by Nadia, their new residential assistant and nurse. She was a fantastic girl, and Claire was harbouring secret plans about her and Aaron getting married and having many babies.

It wasn't all sunshine and trips to the allotment, of course. The kids they hosted had seen more horrors in their short lives than most British adults could even imagine. They all had special medical needs, from diabetes to an amputated leg. One little girl had, horrifyingly, been branded on the nape of her neck with what looked like a hot poker. Claire and Michael had, in many ways, been preparing their whole lives for their new roles. In between the two of them, they had over fifty years' experience working with refugees all over Africa and the Middle East. They had spent years working in Hutu camps in Tanzania and Zaire. There was nothing they had not seen, and nothing they had not heard of. In fact, the children seemed to relate to them well.

Claire showed the older ones pictures of what life was like in refugee camps of the eighties and nineties, and she was amazed to find what they were most surprised at was her and Michael's youthful appearance. They also responded well to Michael's brain injury. They asked to see his scar, hidden by the hair that still grew on the side of his head. They weren't frightened or grossed out. In fact, they understood better than most. They all knew someone who had been shot, or badly hurt by a landmine.

In a selfish self-centred way, Claire felt as though the children were healing them more than the other way around. They listened to their war stories, and asked for more again and again. They looked up to Michael in a way his own children had not since he had been shot. They were survivors, and knew about surviving. Claire hoped that this was mutual healing, that her and Michael were not unloading their heavy past on the already overburdened shoulders of these poor children. She hoped that was true as she saw the kids come out of their shells, gently, slowly, and start playing again. She found herself playing with them more than she ever had with her own grandchildren, chasing them around the allotment with a water hose and allowing the two little girls to braid her long grey hair with flowers from the garden.

As she drained the green beans, Aaron put his arm around her. He squeezed her tight and kissed the top of her forehead.

"How's the book, Mum?"

"It's good, actually." That was the other thing. As she was feeling lighter and happier, Claire was feeling inspired. When she had sold the idea of a short book of refugee stories to her publisher, Claire was thinking of a quick short stocking filler to raise funds for the refuge. However, it had blossomed into something more. For the first time in over a decade, she felt the urge to write.

It wasn't the children's stories, it was stories for the children. It was tales of young princes and princesses who had been stranded in a foreign land, without their mums and dads and aunties and uncles. She knew she risked falling into a cliché: refugee children notoriously make for excellent characters, from *The Chronicles of Narnia* to *The Railway Children*. And yet she could not help herself, and woke up earlier and earlier in the morning to get a few hours of writing done before everyone else got out of bed.

Aaron was often up with her, bringing her cups of coffee and rubbing her shoulder as she typed away at her outdated keyboard. For the first time in her writing career she had no deadline, and yet she worked as though she did. She had a glint in her eye and a spring in her step. She typed with rhythm and gusto. Words flew straight from her mind onto the page, and compounded into sentences, which piled up into paragraphs, which made entire chapters out of thin air. After many years, she felt she was back.

"Mum?" Aaron whispered.

"Yes, darling?"

"I love you." He never said that, not out loud. She had never needed him to.

She smiled, softly. "I love you too, baby."

There was a bang at the door. Someone yelled out her name. The thumping of feet. The rustling of bags. The children were home.

23

ALEX AND SARAH

They met by chance, at the wine bar that connects the two halves of the Logan airport food court in Boston. He was waiting for his flight to Washington, where he was headed for a two-day meeting with a client. She was on a layover, from Zurich back home to San Francisco. They were sat at the bar and spotted each other under the brightly coloured TVs that were showing the Red Sox game. It had been five years since they had sold the flat they used to own together in Canary Wharf.

They briefly considered pretending they hadn't seen each other, but quickly realised there was no real escape. She smiled and lifted three fingers from the counter in a shy greeting. He waved, ducked to collect his coat and briefcase and walked around to join her at the other side of the bar. They hugged, stiffly, each very conscious of the other's body. They both knew everything about each other, thanks to Facebook and their many common friends. It was awkward to admit they had kept tabs on each other. They had not spoken in person since that last stunted phone call, weeks after their final argument.

"What are you doing here?" she asked, rather stupidly. *Of*

course, she thought, *he must be catching a flight. He lives in Boston now, this is clearly his airport.*

§&

He smiled. "Just off to Washington last-minute for a couple of days. Clients," he added, rolling his eyes. He knew she would remember his demanding and capricious clients, how he lived at their beck and call. Of course, much less so now he was in a senior role and had moved to a smaller, more family-oriented firm. The money was nowhere near as good and the clients were nowhere near as interesting, but he was home every day by six and did not have to send a single email at the weekends, unless he wanted to.

§&

She spotted his golden wedding band on his ring finger. She wondered whether his wife minded, him taking off at short notice like that. Leaving her alone with the kids, with no time to organise a babysitter.

§&

He looked over at her wedding band, small and silver, sitting neatly beside an impressive engagement ring. He thought back to the photos of her wedding he had seen online. It was at a vineyard in Napa Valley, surrounded by picturesque rows of olive trees. She had worn a white satin jumpsuit, and had a bouquet of vine leaves. It had been so beautiful it had made it into a wedding magazine. For someone who always claimed to have no interest in weddings, Sarah had by all accounts organised a truly magical day.

Quite a few of their London friends had attended, and a couple had stopped over to visit him in Boston on the way back from San Francisco. He had only recently moved up to Boston from New York, and he and Rita were still refurbishing the house. The visitors were crammed on two air mattresses in the lounge, and had been awakened in the early hours of the morning by the twins, who were only six months old at the time and required their breakfast before dawn.

"How are your children?" Sarah asked. She would never cease to surprise him, with her ability to read his mind.

"They're great," he replied, lighting up. "They've just turned three and it's such a great age!" Alex tried to be careful with his words. He knew she didn't have any kids, at least not yet. It could be infertility, a sore subject. He did not want to rub it in. He who had not wanted kids, blessed with twins. She who had wanted them enough to uproot their whole lives together, still nothing.

Sarah saw a cloud go over his face as he mentioned his children. *He must wonder what life could have been like if I'd said yes when he asked me to come to New York and start a family,* she thought. She had felt deeply relieved when she'd found out he and his new girlfriend were expecting. The rumour on the grapevine was that it had been an accident, that she had gotten pregnant by mistake and could not bring herself to have an abortion. Sarah suspected otherwise. She thought those children were planned, and very much wanted.

Alex had wanted a family badly enough to end their relationship, he must have decided it was time to look elsewhere for the mother of his children. Rita, according to mutual friends, was a curvy and bubbly blonde from his office. They had started dating casually, and suddenly she had fallen pregnant. They had moved to Boston to be close to her family, and he had found a much less demanding job that allowed him to still have a career in finance while raising his children. That was the life he must have dreamed of when he had first asked Sarah to move to America with him.

They kept chatting and drinking for a few minutes.

"So," he said, "San Francisco. How did you end up there?"

She smiled. "Do you remember my horrible boss, Lewis?"

Of course he remembered. The man was a twit, and a sexist.

"It turns out he was not actually horrible. He was just given really bad direction from management, and had to do a lot of things he did not want to do. Like giving me that terrible wedding account." She smiled. She had actually been very grateful for all the work she had done on the wedding gown client when it came to planning her own wedding, with only two months' notice and Homeland Security breathing down her neck.

"At any rate, about a year after you... left," it was still awkward to mention Alex leaving, "he decided to start his own marketing firm in San Francisco. He had a lot of contacts there, and asked me if I would like to come with him as a minority partner." She had not even needed time to think about it, she had said yes there and then, in the lift where he had asked her. Things had ended with Steve a few months prior, as she knew they were not going anywhere. She was still living with her sister and ready to move.

"That's amazing!" Alex seemed genuinely thrilled for her. "What is it like, having your own firm?"

She shook her head, taking a big gulp from her wine glass. She had to start gathering her things, her gate would be announced soon. "I don't work there anymore, actually. We got bought out after a year or so. Thankfully I got to marry my husband and stay in the country." That was a slightly misleading description of what had happened. That evening, she had met up with Vin for dinner, and had told him the news. They were getting bought out, which was financially good news but meant she would have to leave the US. They had only been dating for about a year, but he did not hesitate. She must stay, he'd said. They must get married so she could stay. She had shaken her head with a sad smile. She was over visa weddings. Vin said he understood. Sarah had told him everything about what had happened with Alex, and he knew how hard it was for her to find herself in the same situation again.

She had gone home that night desperately thinking of ways to stay in the country. She had turned the key in her apartment, only to find Vin inside, ready to propose for real.

"Don't marry me for the Green Card," he'd said with a serious look on his face. "Marry me because I love you."

She'd said yes, immediately, and immediately regretted it. It was too soon, it was far too soon. She had a hard time trusting men, she explained to Vin. She had a hard time trusting that the life they were building together was for real. He'd said nothing, and booked himself an appointment for a vasectomy.

At first, she'd thought he was mentally unstable. She told him to cancel his appointment. He refused. She asked if she could go with him. He said yes. They sat in the waiting room, holding hands. She had never heard of a grand romantic gesture taking place in a urologist's office, and yet there they were. Once he got out, limping and smiling, she asked him whether he would rather get married on the coast or in Napa Valley. He'd kissed her in the parking lot and said he didn't mind, as long as he got to be her husband.

"How about you?" she asked to shift the conversation. "How did you meet your wife?" It was a slightly personal question, but she could not help herself.

"She was just a friend from work," he replied quickly. That was true. It was also true that they had started dating with the very clear provision that it would not be a serious relationship. Then, they had decided to go for tacos on a Saturday afternoon. Such a small decision can change your whole life. She'd had a bad fish taco and was sick. The day after she was fine, and they'd had a fun Sunday in bed. In hindsight, of course being sick had made her birth control ineffective. And three weeks later they had both held each other and cried, while Rita clutched a blazing positive pregnancy test.

She had wanted to get an abortion, and he had been relieved. He did not want to feel as though he was pressuring her into it, but she was very determined that this minor bump in the road would not derail her life plans. She wanted to travel, see the world. She wanted to be the youngest woman in New York to make partner at a wealth management firm. However, she simply could not go through with it. She went down to Planned Parenthood three times, once with Alex, once with her best friend and once alone. She just couldn't, she'd told him.

And then, he had gone with her to the scan. It took him a few minutes to realise that those two pulsating blobs on the screen were people, children, his own children. He started crying, big embarrassing sobs as Rita and the nurse tried to comfort him. Something changed on that day. He could see Rita as someone's mum, wearing tight jeans on her curvy figure and tying her blonde hair up in a ponytail. Imagining her as a mother made him fall in love with her. Imagining his children looking like her made him love them too. He could not explain it, but he felt fiercely determined to love and protect them. They were a part of him and had not asked to be brought into this world. He owed them a happy life.

Alex asked Rita to marry him on a walk on The High Line, while they were eating ice cream and making fun of tourists. She said yes, and two weeks later they got married at the New York City Hall on a sunny Wednesday morning. They didn't turn up to the office that day. Somehow, they could not bring themselves to care about work as much as they used to.

"She was a colleague," he repeated. "And I guess we just fell in love."

Sarah smiled. She was so happy for him. She got up, collecting her bags. She explained she had to go. She put her hand on his shoulder, caringly.

"Alex," she said, softly, "I'm so happy you got what you wanted." She kissed him on the cheek and turned round, briskly making her way to her flight. She could not stop smiling. As much as she loved her husband, she would have hated for her happiness to have come at the cost of Alex's.

She was no longer in love with him, but would always care about his feelings. This way, they were both happy. She had her perfect romance with Vin, their tiny loft with views of the Golden Gate Bridge, their late evenings out with friends, their many expensive vacations to exciting places around the world. He had his wife, their boisterous twins and their days out as a family at the zoo or at the beach. She could put that chapter of her life to rest, go home to Vin, kiss him and stroll into the sunset together.

Alex watched Sarah walk off. As always, she was carrying too many things: hand luggage, a briefcase, a jacket and a shopping bag from the duty free. She'd seemed happy, in spite of the fact she didn't have any children. Maybe she'd changed her mind. After all, he had. He very much had. His children were the centre of his world, and he could never imagine his life without them. He smiled thinking about them. He should FaceTime them from the gate before they went to bed.

As he gathered his things, Alex wondered what Sarah had meant by her parting words. His life was nothing like what he had always wanted, and yet he loved it more than he ever thought possible. He shrugged. *I guess I'll never know.*

He picked up his bag and walked towards the gate.

THE END

Printed in Great Britain
by Amazon